IRON WILL

Blood and Iron Series
Book 2

NICK EFSTATHIOU
RON RIPLEY

EDITED BY SCARE STREET

ISBN: 979-8-89476-319-4

Copyright © 2025 by ScareStreet.com

ENTER THE REALM OF TERROR...

We'd like to take a moment to thank you for your support and invite you to join our VIP newsletter.

Dive deeper into the darkness with exclusive offers, early access to new releases, and bone-chilling deals when you sign up at www.ScareStreet.com.

Let the nightmares begin…

See you in the shadows,
Scare Street

CHAPTER 1
A CONVERSATION

The birds sang in Edgewood Cemetery, a fact not unnoticed by Stan Owens.

He sat on the granite steps of Anderson Chapel, a set of black worry beads in his hands. They were a recent gift from Marilyn, his landlady, and they helped ease the thoughts racing through his mind.

The beads, fashioned from some sort of black stone, felt cool and comforting against his fingers. A cold breeze, a harbinger of the seasons to come, rippled through the leaves of the old oaks and elms.

Stan looked out over the headstones and the gentle slope of the cemetery, the wrought iron fence separating the dead from the traffic passing by. He wondered how many, if any, thought of the dead. And of those who did, how many thought of those who still lingered on after death?

From his perch in front of the chapel, Stan could see a handful of ghosts. Some remained by their stones. Others wandered and spoke with one another. One man, in his early twenties, if Stan had to guess, sat on his headstone, a look of confusion on his face.

"I don't think he's accepted it yet," Shane Ryan stated, coming up silently and sitting down a few feet away from Stan.

Stan's heart thumped several times, his body's sole expression of surprise at Shane's sudden appearance.

"I think you are correct in that assessment," Stan remarked. "You are a quiet man."

Shane smiled, shrugged and asked, "Mind if I smoke?"

Stan shook his head.

The other man took out a pack of Lucky Strike cigarettes, shook one out and lit it, his movements quick and sure.

Shane exhaled through his nostrils and then glanced at Stan. "Do you ever go and talk to some of them?"

"Those that are confused?" Stan asked in return.

Shane nodded.

"No. Unless it is absolutely necessary," Stan replied. "I know they must come to it on their own."

"I think it depends."

"On what?" Stan asked.

Shane flashed him a grin, missing more than a few teeth. "That's the question, isn't it? I don't know. I know a kid, though, he seems to always know when a new ghost should be approached."

"Interesting. The kid, he can see them, too?"

"I guess you could say that," Shane said. "He's also on the spectrum. Name is Jimmy Hsu and he's a solid kid. I try not to talk with him too much, though."

Stan frowned. "Why?"

"I've got a bad habit of ruining people I'm around," Shane sighed. He took another drag off the cigarette. "I've got a couple of friends who say that's not true, but they haven't seen the corpses, you know?"

"I do."

Shane looked at him with surprise, then he nodded. "Yeah, I can see you do. So, Stan, you asked to speak to me, and you said you didn't want to do it over the phone, which says a lot. Says everything except what you want to talk about."

"I know, and I do appreciate you coming here to meet me," Stan stated.

Shane laughed. "I've got friends and family buried here. Friends I made after they were buried, mind you. So, it's no skin off my back to come here. Plus, like I said, I live nearby, and I like to walk."

"But you do not even know what I am going to ask," Stan said.

"No," Shane grinned. "But I'm pretty sure I'm going to say okay."

"Really? Why?"

Shane shrugged. "Why not? I've done a lot, Stan. Most of it bad, although it was for a good reason. Kind of weighs on you after a while. I'm kind of hoping you're going to ask for something that I can do that isn't, well, nasty."

Stan nodded in understanding, flashes of his childhood trying to interrupt his thoughts.

"Yes," Stan smiled after a moment. "I am looking for information, Shane."

"Information."

"Yes," Stan confirmed. "As you know, my friend Kenny was killed, and he is buried here, in Edgewood Cemetery. There were two people responsible for his death, the one who killed him and the one who ordered that he be killed."

"Which one are you looking for?" Shane asked, finishing his cigarette.

"I am looking for the man who ordered the killing. The one who did it, a ghost, he is no longer a concern."

"No?" Shane asked.

"No. I destroyed the item he was attached to," Stan stated. "He did not believe I could do it. I disabused him of that opinion."

"Disabused," Shane chuckled. "Very nice. So, who are you looking for?"

Stan reached into the inner pocket of his suit jacket and removed an envelope. He passed it to Shane, who slipped it into the front pocket of the gray sweatshirt he wore. Then, as he waited for Stan to speak, Shane field stripped the cigarette butt and put the remnants into the pocket as well.

"His name, as you will see," Stan began, "is Ezra Pettigrew. He is a businessman, from what I gathered, and he has questionable tactics regarding the making of money."

"Par for the course," Shane muttered.

"So it would seem," Stan agreed. "However, these tactics in Mason centered on the use of ghosts to enforce his will upon his workers. This resulted not only in Kenny's death but in the deaths and abuse of others. A good friend of mine is now in the ICU here in Nashua because of the attack."

Anger flickered across Shane's face. "What sort of information do you want on this guy, Pettigrew?"

"Whatever you might be able to find," Stan answered.

"Then I'll find it," Shane stated. "And if I can't, well, I know people who are a helluva lot better with the internet than I am. I'll send you along to them. One way or another, we'll get you the information you need."

"Thank you."

Shane nodded, took out his cigarettes and looked over the cemetery with a growing smile.

"What is it?" Stan asked.

"I was getting bored at home," Shane answered. "Now, I'm not."

Stan nodded.

He understood how the Marine felt. It was always better to be doing something. Especially when that something was hunting down someone who needed killing.

CHAPTER 2
NEW OFFICES

Ezra Pettigrew shut the treadmill down, stepped off the machine, and took his towel from the bar. For a moment, he stood, mopped the sweat off his brow and the back of his neck, and disliked growing old.

A knock at the door to his small, private gym startled him, and he called out, "Come in."

He watched through the mirror as the door opened, and Robert, his assistant, entered. The man set a freshly mixed smoothie on a table and then came in several more steps.

"Good morning, sir," Robert greeted. "How was your sleep?"

"Better," Ezra smiled. "Thank you for the drink, Robert."

"Of course, sir."

"Are you settled in now?"

"I am, sir," Robert nodded. "As is Abigail. These offices are much larger and far more conducive to work."

"I'm glad to hear it." Ezra tossed his towel into the hamper by the treadmill and walked to the smoothie. Robert stepped to one side and waited.

Ezra lifted the drink, took a sip, and smiled. "I am always impressed with your ability to make this not only edible, but tasty, Robert. Well done."

Robert inclined his head slightly. "You are quite welcome."

Ezra sat down, crossed one leg over the other, and asked, "You have something to tell me? You look bothered."

"Some unpleasant searches, I'm afraid," Robert answered.

Ezra frowned, then motioned for Robert to sit, which he did.

"Tell me," Ezra began. "What are these unpleasant searches about?"

"Primarily you, sir," Robert stated. "We're getting a lot of hits from various search engines seeking information about you."

"You're sure of this?" Ezra asked, disliking the chill racing through him.

"Very much so, sir. These searches are becoming narrower."

"Explain."

"First, general inquiries," Robert said. "Your last name, the facility in New Hampshire. Then your last name and first name as well as a blank search for other companies you were associated with."

"But we sold the facility in New Hampshire and scrubbed the records, correct?" Ezra asked.

Robert nodded. "We did. It doesn't mean that additional digging, especially via the Darkweb, won't give up information we don't want shared."

"Is there a way to remove it completely?"

Robert shook his head. "We can hide it, bury it, but there will always be some sort of record. What we can do is attempt to redirect searches."

"Can you do that?"

"I'm afraid not, sir," Robert said with an apologetic smile. "I can find someone, however, who can. May I suggest we also ask that other names be redirected?"

"You may," Ezra nodded, taking a sip. "Why, though?"

"Information is a resource," Robert explained. "Should there be only one person, meaning you, that we are attempting to redirect inquiries away from, the contractor may realize he or she has potential currency."

"Blackmail?" The word tasted foul in Ezra's mouth.

Robert shook his head. "That generally requires too much interaction with the victim and inevitably leads to discovery. What is more likely is someone will post that a certain individual is looking to have their information hidden. This will lead others to do further research with the aim to either blackmail you or sell the information to those seeking it."

"And should we have a group of people we want redirected?" Ezra inquired.

"If we put out a contract for a group, say twenty to thirty people, all in the same general type of work, the contractor won't see it as profitable to list them singly or as a group," Robert stated. "Instead, the money for the group should keep the contractor focused on the redirection efforts."

"Paying them more just for me wouldn't work?" Ezra asked.

"No, sir. It would only show desperation and the ability to be taken advantage of." Robert smiled. "While we both know neither of those applies to you, sir, it would be much better to not engage in any unnecessary interactions with the contractor, whomever we choose to go with."

"You've made your case, Robert," Ezra smiled. "Do as you see fit regarding the redirection."

"Very good, sir," Robert said, getting to his feet.

Ezra raised his glass in salute, and Robert left the room.

As the door clicked closed, Ezra took a long drink. The sudden search for him online was disturbing. It meant that somehow, someone knew who he was in New Hampshire.

Leaning over, Ezra pushed the call button for Abigail.

The middle aged woman entered a few minutes later. She was a no-nonsense type of person and wore little, if any, makeup. Her graying brown hair was pulled back into a loose ponytail, and small ruby earrings hung in her ears. The woman rarely smiled, but that was because of her focus on whatever task was at hand and not a hint at her personality.

Ezra had known Abigail for fifteen years, and every one of them had been a delight.

She looked at the drink, then the treadmill and then at him.

"You're finally taking the doctor's advice?" she asked.

"I am," Ezra chuckled. "Would you care to sit?"

She nodded and took the seat recently vacated by Robert.

"Robert says you are settling in?"

"I am," Abigail replied. "This is a comfortable area. Plenty of shops downtown and even a few museums. Easy access to the airport, as well as train stations. While the town is not a hub of activity, it is within easy commuting distance."

"Well," Ezra said, finishing his drink, "you and Robert are the ones who picked and established this place. Thank you for that."

She smiled and nodded. "Is there anything I can do for you, sir?"

"There is," Ezra stated. "I would like you to follow up with James Beckinsale. Make certain he's doing well. Also, see if you can find an inexpensive home in the Concord, New Hampshire region."

"Any particular name I should use for that purchase?" she asked.

"No. Create a new persona or company for this one, please," Ezra stated. "I don't want too much out there under anything recognizable."

"Of course, sir," she smiled. "Is there anything else I can do for you?"

He shook his head. "No, Abigail, that is all for now. Thank you for your assistance."

She smiled and left the room.

Ezra sat in the silence, finished his drink, and wondered who had the gall to try and hunt him down.

CHAPTER 3
PHILOMENA AND ADAM

"You appear disturbed."

Stan didn't respond to Philomena as his dead grand aunt appeared on the other side of the buried salt barrier.

She frowned. "Have you merely come to gloat, or is there a reason for your visit today, Stan?"

"There is a reason," Stan stated. He clasped his hands behind his back and looked at the dead woman. "I have questions regarding your late husband's business."

Philomena snorted. "I did not want to know about it, and so I did my best not to."

"You were aware of your husband's business," Stan continued. "You were also well aware of the funds which kept the home, as you were wont to say, in the black."

A wicked smile crept onto her face.

"Yes, I did say that. More than a little too often. You are correct," she nodded. "I am confused. You have the money. What else is there to know?"

"The properties," Stan told her. "I may need to put them to use. I did so with the Cellar Hole, but I am concerned about awakening any of the dead who we buried there. I would rather they rest and not remember their suffering."

Philomena shook her head. "How you managed to survive my husband, I will never know. I thought for certain he would have stamped any sort of kindness out of you. Or at least killed you as he tried."

"How many properties are there?" Stan asked, refusing to remember the brutalities he had suffered.

Philomena closed her eyes, then said, "I believe fourteen, although I am not completely sure."

She opened her eyes and looked at him. "There is an old vault hidden in Cellar Hole. He told me of it once when he was too drunk to beat me or do anything else, for that matter. In the left-hand corner, you will find a brick with the image of an upside-down rat stamped into it. Should you be able to work that brick out of the wall after all these years, you'll find a pull. Give that a tug, and the door should open."

"What is in the vault?" Stan asked.

"I don't know," she replied. "He only bragged that there were deeds to the properties there and other things he liked to keep hidden."

Stan repressed a shiver. In his youth, he been intimately familiar with the things his granduncle had enjoyed keeping hidden.

"Thank you, Philomena," Stan finally said. "I will go to the Cellar Hole soon."

"You'll tell me what you find?"

The notes of genuine hope and curiosity in her voice caused him to look at her. "If you wish it."

Her face tightened. "I am bored, Stanley Owens. I do not particularly appreciate your company, but some company is better than none."

He gave a short nod. "You are quite right, Philomena. When I learn what is in the vault, I will come and speak with you. Maybe tomorrow."

"Why won't you go today?" she asked as he started to turn away.

He paused. "My friend, Adam, is in the hospital. He was beaten badly by ghosts. I will go and check on him, and when I am done there, and if there is nothing pressing that needs doing, I will go and inspect the vault."

"What happened to the ghost?" Philomena asked, her voice sharp. "The one who killed my godson?"

"I forgot to tell you," Stan remembered. "I apologize, Philomena. I destroyed him. In the Cellar Hole."

"How?"

"I burned him," Stan answered. "It was the worst I could have done."

"How is that the worst?" she asked.

"Because he had originally died by fire," Stan told her.

He turned away and started down the long driveway back to the road.

Philomena spoke as he walked, and her words haunted him back to Marilyn's. "Your grand uncle would have been proud."

✳ ✳ ✳

Adam lay in the bed, and the room looked cold.

Stan gazed at his young friend, at the tubes in his mouth and the IV in his hand, and wondered if Adam would wake.

No one could tell him. It was, according to the doctor, the proverbial waiting game.

Again, Stan looked around the room and decided it needed some form of decoration.

Standing up, he left the room, passed by the nurse's station quietly enough so that neither of the nurses noticed him, and made his way to the stairs. He walked down several flights to the lobby and stepped out into a hallway that had more people than he cared to see.

He crossed the hall and entered the gift shop, nodding hello to an older woman who greeted him as he crossed the threshold.

"May I help you find anything?" she asked.

Stan forced a smile. "No, thank you."

He turned his back to the woman at what he hoped was an acceptable speed and let his eyes wander the displays. It took him a moment, but he soon saw a dark brown stuffed teddy bear on a shelf.

The plastic eyes, which did not look real, stared out into nothingness, but Stan found the toy to be comforting. He walked to it, took the bear down and nodded at the softness of the fur. The toy would be just right for the room.

Stan turned around and strode to the counter, placing the bear down in front of the woman.

"That was quick," she stated, adjusting the narrow-framed glasses she wore as she picked the bear up. She frowned, turned it over and then uttered, "Ha!"

Stan watched as she rang up the price, thirty-two dollars, and then he extracted the exact sum from his wallet.

"Not many folks pay with cash anymore," the woman remarked, ringing up the sale.

Stan forced another smile.

She closed the cash drawer, printed a receipt and then handed it to him. "Would you like a bag?"

"No, thank you," Stan replied.

"For a little person?"

Stan frowned. "What do you mean?"

"A child," she clarified. "Do you have a child here? A young relative?"

"I have a younger friend in the ICU," Stan stated. "His room is bare, and I believe this will liven it up a little."

"That is very kind of you," the woman smiled. "I'm sure his parents will appreciate it, too."

"That I do not know," Stan told her. "I am not even certain they are alive."

The look of surprise on the woman's face followed him out of the gift shop.

He took a single step toward the stairwell when his stomach rumbled, and he caught the scent of a BLT. Stan paused, saw a small cafe and walked toward it. He found several refrigerators of pre-packaged sandwiches and salads, drinks and fruits. A small counter held the cash register and a place to order a limited variety of hot sandwiches.

A young man, who looked as though he would rather be anywhere than behind the register, smiled wanly at Stan.

"What can I get for you?" the young man asked, sweeping his purple-dyed hair out of his eyes.

"A BLT, please," Stan answered.

The young man nodded, audibly repressed a sigh, and turned away to call someone from a back room of the small kitchen.

"Stan? Stan Owens?"

Turning around, Stan saw a woman his own age standing a few feet behind him. In her hands, she held a pre-packaged salad and sparkling water. She wore a black suit with a purple dress shirt, and her graying black hair was cut fashionably short.

He blinked, and the first genuine smile in a long time found its way onto his face.

"Gwen Leigh," Stan said. "I have not seen you since high school."

"And that was longer ago than I'd like to admit," she replied. "It's great bumping into you like this."

"It is great to see you, too."

"Do you have a few minutes to catch up?"

Stan nodded, feeling a flush creep up his neck and cheeks.

CHAPTER 4
BACK-UPS AND SYSTEM CHECKS

"You're certain of this?" Ezra asked, more out of habit than any real doubt.

"Yes," Robert nodded. "I have been able to confirm from several sources that the person seeking information from you is located in Southern New Hampshire."

Ezra frowned. "We can't narrow it down any further?"

Robert shook his head. "Not without making a lot of noise about it, and that might tip off whoever it is. From what our contractor stated, the search is fairly generic. He was quick to add it doesn't mean there aren't any traps set up."

"Traps?" Ezra's frown deepened.

"Yes, sir. Apparently, some of the more skilled contractors and users can leave behind trackers hidden in code that will lead them back directly to the original searcher."

"Triggering such a trap would lead to our contractor, correct?" Ezra asked. "We are still protected?"

"Yes," Robert confirmed. "It's why we went with a private contractor and a group package."

"Hmm." Ezra rubbed at the stubble on his chin for a moment. "Thank you, Robert, for the update."

"Of course, sir." Robert looked at him and asked, "Is there anything else you need?"

"No," Ezra smiled. "It's after five. You should have left earlier."

Robert nodded. "I was waiting on this response, sir. I felt it was important."

"Still," Ezra sighed. "Make a note of it, please."

"Yes, sir."

Once Robert left the room, Ezra brought up his private calendar and made a note to increase Robert's New Year's bonus.

With that done, he leaned back in his chair and looked up at the white ceiling of his office. Someone was looking for him. Someone from Southern New Hampshire. This could only be because of the facility and the deaths that had resulted from the ghosts. There could be several individuals responsible for the search, but he suspected it was Stanley Owens.

Ezra frowned at the idea of it.

Owens had struck him as a country bumpkin. Skilled with the dead, but that was all. Hell, the man didn't even have his own home. He ate at a diner and lived in a single room at a boarding house. Owens didn't seem to be especially competent in anything other than scrapping with the dead.

Still, it didn't mean he hadn't gotten some sort of assistance. Maybe there was someone younger, or at least smarter when it came to computers, who was lending him a hand.

For a moment, Ezra considered assassinating Stanley Owens, but such an act could go bad quickly. No, he would need to resort to intimidation. Some form that wouldn't directly be traced back to him.

A slow smile spread across his face. He would use the dead again. There had been notable successes when he had the first time, and had James Beckinsale not been so painfully injured, Ezra's business plan would have succeeded.

Now, there was no need to worry about a facility or making money from it. Ezra had cut his losses from that fiasco, and so employing the dead as a tool against Stanley Owens would be more than acceptable.

Except, he couldn't go directly against Owens. Not with the dead. He would need another way.

Owens was well-liked in town. A man whom everyone appreciated and spoke with. Would that appreciation and familiarity remain if he became the reason people were attacked? Would that turn Owens into a pariah?

One could only hope.

"Methuselah," Ezra murmured to himself. With a smile, he picked up his phone and dialed the number.

✳ ✳ ✳

Morrigan let the phone ring three times and then answered it as the last ring finished.

She brought the heavy handset to her ear and waited.

"Methuselah," a man stated.

Morrigan smiled. "Has done the surprising. He has gone and died."

There was a pause, but much briefer than others she had encountered.

"New management, then?" the voice inquired.

"Indeed."

He chuckled. "May I ask with whom I am speaking?"

"My name is Morrigan."

"Ms. Morrigan," he started.

"Morrigan, nothing more," she interrupted.

"My apologies, Morrigan. I am looking to acquire some items," he told her.

She sat down at her desk, took up her pen and jotted down the date on a fresh page of her yellow legal pad. "May I have a name?"

"I am Mr. Pettigrew," he answered.

"Excellent, Mr. Pettigrew," Morrigan smiled, writing the name down. "Tell me, what are you looking for?"

"I'm looking for items that were once owned by people who were comfortable with violence."

Morrigan added *Level 4* beneath Pettigrew's name. "How many?"

she asked.

He hesitated before answering. "Three. Three to begin with."

She added that number to the growing list of information. "Do you have a mailing address?"

"Not yet," he replied.

Morrigan frowned. "I cannot reserve items."

"Nor do I expect you to."

She grinned. "Good. Cellphone number?"

Pettigrew told her, and she added it to everything else. When she finished, she set the pen down and said, "When I find three that are suitable to your needs, I will text you. When you receive the text, call me back. Leave a message if I do not answer. I will return your call within ten hours."

"Excellent."

"Be sure to have your phone on, Mr. Pettigrew," she informed him. "It is the best way to ensure you have the items you want."

He chuckled. "I will leave my cell phone on, Morrigan. Thank you."

They said goodbye, and the call ended.

Morrigan stood up and stretched her back. She had an hour before her next observation. Plenty of time to browse the shelves and see what might fit Mr. Pettigrew's needs.

CHAPTER 5

OUTSIDE THE VFW

Reminiscing with Gwen Leigh had been more than Stan could have hoped for. She was the same bright and witty person he remembered from high school, only older and more mature. And, if he was honest with himself, stunningly attractive.

In his small notebook, Stan had Gwen's phone number, and she had Marilyn's number in her cellphone's address book. Gwen had thought it too funny that he didn't have a cellphone.

"We're here," the cab driver stated.

Stan blinked and looked out the car window. He saw the Milford VFW and nodded. He paid the driver and exited the car. As it pulled away, Stan walked toward the building. There were some days when he only felt comfortable among other veterans. Men and women who knew violence.

Stan walked into the VFW and made his way to the bar, taking a seat and nodding to the barman, who was new. As the man approached, Stan took out his wallet, removed his VFW card and held it for the man to inspect.

"Not your chapter," the barman remarked, nodding for Stan to put it away.

"It is not," Stan confirmed.

The barman, who appeared old enough to have served in the First Iraq War, grunted in disapproval. Still, he could not turn Stan away.

"What'll you have?"

"A double shot of whatever your top-shelf vodka is," Stan answered. "And then a pitcher of Heineken."

The man raised an eyebrow. "Are you driving?"

Stan shook his head. "I am not."

"How are you getting home?"

"I have a cab scheduled to pick me up at seven."

For the first time, the barman did something other than frown or glare. A smile flickered across his face. "Hell, that's more than most of the people here even think to do."

The barman got Stan his drinks, set them down on the counter, wiped his hand off his shirt and offered it. "Name's Patrick."

"Stan," he replied and shook the hand.

"A pleasure," Patrick stated. "Sorry about the interrogation. Sometimes, we get people in here who try to drink for cheap."

"I understand."

"Do you want to run a tab?" Patrick asked.

Stan shook his head. "That would be an unwise decision on my part. I will pay for these drinks, and that will be my limit."

"Sure thing," Patrick nodded and told Stan the price.

Stan pulled out his wallet, counted out the bills, plus a healthy-sized tip, and gave it to Patrick.

The barman grinned. "You know, that's what I like about the older guys. It's cash. Always cash."

Stan nodded. "No one needs to know."

"Exactly!" Patrick laughed, sweeping his blonde hair away from his brow. "Exactly. Anyway, give me a holler if you need anything. I'll be patrolling the bar."

"Thank you."

Stan focused on his drinks as the barman walked away.

The vodka went down easy, and the beer like water. Stan let his thoughts wander, and he paid no mind to the conversations around him. By the time he was halfway through the pitcher, he noticed the crowd in the bar had grown and that a single man was glaring at him.

Stan poured himself another beer and ignored the stranger.

The stranger, however, didn't want to be ignored.

From the corner of his eye, Stan watched the much younger man finish a shot, stand and then walk to stop beside Stan.

"Patty says you're not part of this chapter," the man stated, his voice low and thick.

Stan didn't respond. He continued drinking his beer.

"Hey," the stranger growled. "I'm talking to you."

Stan finished the beer and poured the last from the pitcher into his mug.

"Bert," Patrick said, coming closer. "Give it a rest. I was making conversation, not asking you to throw him out."

"He'd better talk, or he's getting thrown out," Bert snarled.

"You ain't on the clock yet," Patrick stated. "Once you start your shift at the door, then you can decide who stays and who goes. Until then, sit and enjoy your drink."

Bert jabbed a finger at Stan, and Stan caught it easily, bending the digit straight back and sending Bert crashing to his knees and howling in pain.

For the first time, Stan looked at Bert. The man was larger than him, easily six and a half feet. He had the mass to go with his height, and from the way he writhed, Stan could see the man worked out on a regular basis.

Bert swore, tried to get to his feet, and Stan bent the finger further back.

"I will break this," Stan informed the man, pausing to take a drink. "It does not matter to me. Patrick has asked you to let it go. I ignored you until I could no longer do so safely."

The bar was quiet.

"I have no doubt you are popular here," Stan continued. "Nor do I doubt you will continue to be popular after I leave. However, should you push this, I will harm you, and you will not enjoy the experience."

Stan looked to Patrick. "If I let him up and he attacks, what will I do?"

Patrick frowned as he glanced from Stan to Bert.

"Hell, Bert," Patrick grumbled. "If you're fool enough to swing at this guy, you'll get what you deserve."

There were additional nods around the bar.

"So be it," Stan stated, and he let go of Bert's finger.

The man attacked.

He was younger and enraged.

Stan was none of those things.

Stan shifted his weight on the stool to allow the first blow to pass him, dipped under the second, and sent a short, sharp jab into the man's solar plexus.

The air rushed out of Bert's lungs as he staggered back, quickly throwing several punches to fend off another blow.

But Stan didn't bother. Instead, he eased off the stool and stepped toward the center of the room. Bert backed into the bar, grabbed the empty pitcher, hurled it at Stan, and charged.

Stan caught the pitcher, saw Bert's eyes widen in surprise, and then smashed the heavy glass into the side of Bert's head.

The younger man went limp and collapsed to the floor.

Stan stepped over Bert and returned the pitcher to the bar.

"Damn," Patrick muttered. He looked at Stan. "You, ah, you've got some skills there, Stan."

"A misspent youth," Stan confessed. "I am hopeful that Bert will be alright. If there is a medic here, however, I would suggest checking him sooner rather than later. I tried not to hit him too hard, but there is always the chance I did."

"We'll check him out," Patrick nodded. "It's not the first time he's gotten into a scrap in here. We generally let it go because this is what happens. Someone gives him a wallop, and he quiets down."

Stan looked at Bert and then asked Patrick, "Did his unit suffer a lot of casualties?"

"Yeah. He saw some heavy stuff," the barman replied. "You know how it is."

"I do," Stan agreed. "Please, let him know that I harbor no ill will toward him. I hope, should we meet again, he will join me for a drink. As it is, my ride should be here."

Without another word, Stan left the room, hopeful that Bert would recover fully.

CHAPTER 6
NEW RECRUITS

Morrigan picked up the phone receiver, set it down, picked it up, set it down, and picked it up a third time.

Always three.

She dialed the number for Mister Ezra Pettigrew, and he answered it on the first ring, bringing a frown to her face.

He should have waited until the third ring.

"Yes?" he asked.

"This is Morrigan. Your items will arrive today at three o'clock."

"Today?"

She heard the surprise in his voice and repressed a smile.

"Yes. There are three of them. All women. They are powerful and will broker no foolishness. Do you understand?"

Pettigrew hesitated, then, in a confused tone he answered, "Yes."

"Call me should there be an issue with any of the dead," Morrigan continued. "However, there should not be. They were chosen for their violence."

At precisely three o'clock in the afternoon, there was a knock on the front door.

Ezra heard it in his office, and a moment later, Robert entered with a small package and a look of concern.

"This was just delivered," he stated, and he showed Ezra the parcel, which had a small label affixed in the upper left hand corner.

The label read:

Morrigan

Fine Antiquities

For the Discerning Collector

Robert shook his head. "No one should know of this place."

"No," Ezra agreed. "They shouldn't."

The fact that Morrigan knew of it caused Ezra some discomfort.

"Is it safe?" Robert asked.

Ezra nodded. "Yes. I was told a package would arrive at three today, but I assumed it would have gone to the address I had given."

"The PO Box."

"Yes," Ezra stated. "The PO Box. I never gave this address. Still, it's here."

Robert looked at it and asked, "Do you want it on your desk, sir, or should we open it in another room?"

"Here," Ezra answered. "And I will open it alone."

"I don't know if that's wise, sir," Robert started.

Ezra smiled. "Robert, if for some reason this is something dangerous, you are not going to be injured simply for being in the same room with me. There would be nothing for you to do except get harmed, and that is not acceptable. You have time coming to you, so please take it and send Abigail home as well. When the two of you are gone, I will open the package."

Robert's face paled. "Do you really think that's wise, sir?"

"I do."

Ezra watched Robert frown, then nod in acquiescence.

"I will text you both later," Ezra continued. "This will let you know I am well."

"And if we don't hear from you?" Robert asked.

"If you have not heard from me by seven this evening, then you may come and check on me," Ezra answered.

"It might be too late."

"It might," Ezra agreed. "But there are certain things that cannot be helped. This is one of them."

"Alright, sir," Robert sighed. "Abigail and I will wait for your message."

"Thank you."

Ezra watched Robert leave the room and close the door behind him. After several minutes of muffled conversation between Robert and Abigail, Ezra heard them leave. A minute later, a message on Ezra's laptop told him the security system had been armed.

With a deep breath, Ezra stood and brought the package into a small room off his office.

The room had started as a supply closet, but Ezra had retrofitted it to serve as a containment area for the dead. All the precautions he knew of were in place. Lead, salt, and iron, as well as lights with hardwired systems to generators that would ensure the dead wouldn't drain the office, or the building, of its energy. He had even gone so far as to purchase a specially made anti-viral box lined with iron and lead-laced glass to handle haunted items and not be affected.

Ezra closed and sealed the door behind him, reached over the safety line on the floor and walls that showed where the salt was secured, and placed the package into the anti-viral box. Carefully, he managed to open the parcel and remove three separate items from within. He set each down, made certain there was no receipt or any other paper trail, and then opened the first item.

Ezra tore the paper away and found a small, porcelain head, something that might have once graced a doll. An equally small tag identified the head as *Gretchen*. Ezra set the head on the table and moved on to the second. Within a moment, he unwrapped a walnut shell, this one labeled *Shirley*. The final object was slightly larger than the others, a paperweight with a single rose petal encased. This was named *Joan*.

He looked at them for several minutes, trying to decide on how best to speak with them. Finally, he turned off one set of lights, allowing a dark shadow to form at the back of the room.

"Hello," Ezra said. "My name is Ezra Pettigrew and I have purchased your items from the dealer."

The darkness at the back of the room shimmered.

"We were told to tell you we're violent," a woman stated.

He raised an eyebrow. "Is it true, or were you told to lie?"

She chuckled. "It's true. My name is Shirley. I murdered seven men and was about to finish off the eighth when I choked to death at dinner."

"I'm Joan," another ghost said, introducing herself. "I was not overly fond of children suffering from the colic. I worked in a hospital in Boston and silenced quite a few before they fired me. They suspected me but never proved it."

"And I'm Gretchen," stated the third and final ghost. "I killed police officers."

The other dead women laughed, and Stan couldn't help but blink in surprise before he asked, "Police officers?"

"All around southern Massachusetts," Gretchen sighed. "I would stalk them and hunt them. Finally, when I knew they would be alone, I was a damsel in distress. They came, and they rescued me. They were, for a short time, knights in shining armor. I slew them each as I gave them their reward."

"And now you're here to kill for me," Ezra stated.

He took their silence as understanding, if not agreement.

"I will send you out soon," he told them. "There will be a place that needs to be disciplined, if you will. A place where the people need to be afraid. And where some will need to die. Perhaps one or two. Just to set the mood."

He looked into the darkest part of the shadow.

"Can you do that?" he asked. "Can you scare them?"

"Mr. Pettigrew," Gretchen murmured, "we can terrify them."

CHAPTER 7
MEMORIES OF BOSTON

Stan sat on an antique Victorian folding chair in a small house on Maple Street.

The house, no larger than 800 square feet, had been one of his granduncle's many properties throughout Southern New Hampshire and Northern Massachusetts. This particular home, located on Maple Street in Mason, had been occupied by the daughter of one of his granduncle's consorts. The woman had passed away two years earlier, and Stan had left it the way it was.

Photographs of the dead woman's relatives still stood on the mantle of the small fireplace, and dishes were still stacked in the cabinets. Her bed, a narrow twin, remained made and ready for the evening.

Twice a week, Annabelle Kelly came in and scoured the house from top to bottom. Annabelle's husband, a retired Marine, had committed suicide 18 months earlier, and she considered the few cleaning jobs a godsend. Marilyn had found them for Annabelle, and Stan had hired her to clean this house, albeit through a third party.

He did not want Marilyn to know he owned the home or any of the others he was learning of. It might damage their friendship, and he did not want to move out of Marilyn's home.

He was safe there, and the people of Mason knew where to find him when he was needed.

But there were times when he needed silence, a place to contemplate past acts and future deeds. At times, the Cellar Hole had served that purpose. Unfortunately, it was also a painful reminder of what had been done to him as a boy.

He had returned to the Cellar Hole after speaking with his grandaunt, and true to the directions she had given him, he had found the vault. He would return to it at some point, but at that time, he had only taken the box with the property deeds.

The house on Maple Street had been one of them.

Stan's eyes shifted to the battered steel box he had extracted from the vault and thought, for a moment, about the deeds contained within it. He wondered how many had been occupied by former consorts, or loyal "soldiers" as his granduncle's men had called themselves.

But they hadn't been soldiers. They had been brutes who had excelled in undisciplined violence, much as Stan had before he enlisted in the Army, where he had learned about real soldiers.

Still, the memories of those years before the Army, of those years being taught violently by his granduncle and the man's soldiers, were never far from his thoughts.

Stan closed his eyes and folded his hands in his lap. The memories pushed against him, and he let them out, knowing that to fight them would inflict more nightmares on his already troubled sleep.

And so, Stan remembered.

✷ ✷ ✷

Eamon O'Leary was a man who liked redheaded women and cheap whiskey. He smoked a seemingly endless chain of cigars and controlled his section of Boston's South End with an iron fist. His mercy extended to small children, dogs, and attractive redheads.

Everyone else suffered.

His loyal troops fashioned themselves after the IRA, and they demanded tribute wherever they went, even when they shouldn't.

And that was why Stan, at thirteen, was in Boston.

Norbert La France parked the car and looked at Stan with his one good eye. "You ready, kid?"

Stan slipped the brass knuckles out of his jacket pockets and fitted them on. "Yes."

"Do you remember what *he* said?"

Stan nodded. All his granduncle's soldiers emphasized the 'he' whenever they spoke, as if the man were a deity.

And perhaps he was to them. A great and terrible beast who could tear them apart.

Which, Stan realized, the man could do. Stan had, in fact, watched and participated in such actions himself. The fear and horror attached to those memories were quickly smothered as he looked past Norbert to the building.

"What is the building again?" Stan asked.

"It's called a rectory," Norbert explained. "Catholic priests live in 'em."

"This man, Eamon, he is a Catholic priest?"

Norbert chuckled and shook his head as he took out a Marlboro and lit it. "No, nothing like that, Stan. He just spends most of his time there. Irish cops in Boston won't go into a rectory, and they won't let anybody else do it, either."

Stan nodded, then pulled his knit cap down lower on his shaved head.

"What are you going to do?" Norbert asked.

"I will cross the street and enter the alley on the left," Stan recited. "I will turn right at the end of the alley and approach the rectory from the back. There will be a large, green door with a golden harp painted upon it. I will knock three times, pause and then knock twice. My hands will go into my pockets to hide the brass knuckles. When the door opens, I will enter, and I will be searched. They will not be concerned with my brass knuckles, only knives and guns. I will not have either."

"How many men?" Norbert asked.

"There will be two in the kitchen, a third in the parlor. One more at the top of the stairs. If Eamon is with a woman, I will be made to wait in a bedroom across from his office. When he is finished, I will be sent into the room."

Norbert nodded, then sighed as he turned and looked out his window.

"Tell me," Norbert continued without looking back at Stan. "What will you do when you are in the office?"

"I have been tasked with sending a message to Eamon and any of those he works with. This message will translate to, 'Do as you're told.'" Stan paused, adjusted his hands in the brass knuckles and added, "I will speak in violence. Should I need to use it, there is a secret door in the closet of Eamon's office that leads to a servant's passage. I will be able to take this to the basement and then exit via a coal chute that opens onto the right alley."

"How long will you take?" Norbert asked.

"As long as needed," Stan answered.

"Get to it, then."

Stan nodded and exited the car.

He crossed the street, walked down the length of the alley and turned right at the end. He saw the back of the building, the green door with the gold harp upon it, and walked to it. He climbed the half-dozen steps and knocked exactly as he had been told.

The door opened almost a minute later, and a pale man with a shock of black hair looked down at Stan, a cigarette dangling from the corner of his mouth.

"You're the messenger?" the man asked in a thick Boston accent.

"Yes."

The man chuckled and motioned for Stan to come in.

Stan did so.

A second man sat at a large round table, a newspaper in front of him and a glass of beer in his hand. He glanced at Stan and then ignored him.

"Spread 'em," the first man ordered, and Stan took his hands out of his pockets. One of the man's eyebrows lifted at the sight of the brass knuckles, but he only chuckled. "Oi, Peter, get a load of these."

Peter, the man at the table, glanced up and saw the brass. He chuckled and asked, "Rough walk, huh?"

Stan nodded as he extended his arms and legs.

"Didn't know they made 'em that small," the first man stated. Still chuckling, he went about his search, which was neither gentle nor rough. He was quick and efficient, and when he was satisfied that Stan wasn't hiding a blade or a firearm, the man straightened up.

"Listen close, little messenger," the first man ordered, and Stan fixed his attention on him. The man nodded approvingly. "Good. Now, you're going to walk down the hall there, and you'll see the main set of stairs. You go straight up those stairs and nowhere else. Do you understand that?"

"Yes."

"Good," the man continued. "Messenger or not, you'll end up in the harbor if you poke your nose where you shouldn't. When you get up to the second floor, there'll be another man standing outside of Mr. O'Leary's office. He's not entertaining this evening, so you shouldn't be kept long. Then you can get back to wherever it is you're from. Understood?"

"Yes."

The man nodded. "Off with you then."

Stan turned away and exited the kitchen. He followed the hallway, passed the parlor where a man sat watching a basketball game on television, and then reached the stairs. He didn't hesitate or deviate from his path, and he continued to the second floor, where a younger man than the first sat on a bench outside Eamon O'Leary's office.

"Sit," the guard ordered, nodding toward a metal folding chair across from him.

Stan did so, his hands in his pockets.

The guard glared at Stan, but Stan paid him no mind. Nothing would distract him from his task.

After several minutes, the guard gave up and crossed his arms over his chest as he leaned against the wall.

A moment later, someone spoke in a language Stan didn't understand, but the guard did.

The man leaped to his feet.

"In you go!" he ordered and opened the door.

Stan got to his feet and entered the office.

The guard shut the door behind him, and Stan looked at the man sitting behind the desk.

"He sent a kid?" Eamon asked, his deep voice reverberating in the room.

"Yes," Stan answered.

Eamon opened a box on his desk, removed a cigar and clipped the end. As he did so, Stan's eyes flickered around the room, taking the entirety of it in. He saw the heavy deadbolt on the door he had entered, how the windows were closed and locked, how the closet door stood open an inch or so, and how Eamon disregarded him.

Stan took a step back toward the door, and Eamon chuckled, misreading the movement.

"How are you related?" Eamon asked.

"He is my granduncle," Stan answered, and he locked the door.

"What the hell are you doing?" Eamon demanded.

Stan sprang toward him, launched over the desk and slammed his right fist into the bridge of Eamon's nose.

Stan delivered the message in less than five minutes, and Eamon was still alive but unconscious. Most of the man's teeth were scattered on the floor, and Stan wondered, for the first time, what the man had done to anger his granduncle.

But as soon as he had the thought, it left.

Stan wiped down his brass knuckles, slid them into his back pocket and took his sweatshirt off, inspecting it closely before he put it back on. He looked at his reflection in a pane of window glass and was glad to see he was free of blood splatter on his face.

Without another look at Eamon O'Leary, Stan went to the closet, opened the secret door, and left the house.

✳ ✳ ✳

Stan opened his eyes and looked around the house on Maple Street.

He disliked the memories of his youth, but if he tried to stop them, his nightmares would be unbearable.

He had forgotten about Eamon O'Leary.

His granduncle had been pleased with the delivery of the message, and it had shown. Stan's own beatings had lessened.

Stan stood up and went into the kitchen. He poured himself a glass of water and considered why he might have remembered O'Leary.

The fight at the VFW.

He had enjoyed the fight as much as he had enjoyed beating Eamon O'Leary.

And Stan felt guilty.

He finished the water and then washed the glass.

It was time to return home.

CHAPTER 8
WINSTON

Winston James Geoffrey Harrington III set his fork down onto his plate, wiped his mouth with the corner of his napkin and picked up his cell phone. He raised an eyebrow at the number on the screen, and then he answered it.

"Good morning."

"Good morning, indeed," Mr. Pettigrew replied. "How are you, Winston?"

"Quite well, sir," Winston remarked. "I returned home from South Africa yesterday."

"Business?"

"Surprisingly, no," Winston chuckled. "Pleasure."

"I'm glad to hear it."

Winston pushed his chair away from the table, lifted his glass of orange juice and took a sip before asking, "To what do I owe the pleasure of this call, Mr. Pettigrew?"

"I was hoping to employ you for a short time. Perhaps a month, perhaps two," Mr. Pettigrew informed him.

"Does it require international travel?"

"No. Just a slight jaunt over the continental US to New Hampshire. Possibly Massachusetts, depending on where you think it best to set up," Mr. Pettigrew stated.

Winston looked at his orange juice, then asked, "What sort of employment?"

Mr. Pettigrew cleared his throat. "It would be delivering packages. Rather mundane work, I'm afraid."

"I don't mind a bit of the mundane now and again," Winston replied. "It makes the other work all the more exciting. Where would I be delivering the packages to?"

"There is a small town in New Hampshire, a place called Mason. These packages would need to be set in specific locations," Mr. Pettigrew stated. "They are of a, well, a supernatural nature."

Winston finished his orange juice, set it on the table, cleared his throat and asked, "A supernatural nature?"

"Yes."

Winston frowned. "As in monsters and such?"

"No," Mr. Pettigrew chuckled, but the sound seemed forced. "Not in the least. They are what you might call cursed or haunted objects."

"Ghosts?"

"Ghosts, indeed," Mr. Pettigrew sighed.

"And that's all the job would entail?" Winston asked. "Placing these items around the town?"

"Yes."

Winston considered the offer. "My usual rate?"

"As if each delivery were a target eliminated," Mr. Pettigrew confirmed. "Accommodations will be provided, as well as a vehicle and a daily stipend."

"And all I have to do is deliver these 'haunted' items to whatever location you dictate?" Winston asked, clarifying the work.

"Yes."

"Are there any dangers associated with these items?" Winston asked.

"There are some, but they are negated with proper safety equipment, which I will provide," Mr. Pettigrew answered.

"This sounds like a sweet deal, Mr. Pettigrew," Winston stated. "Sort of like taking the proverbial candy from a baby. This leads me to my last question on the subject. Why me?"

"I need someone skilled in not being seen," Mr. Pettigrew replied.

"Someone who knows how to get in and out of a place without drawing attention. You would not still be alive if you did not excel at this, Winston."

"Fair enough," Winston said. "Send me the details via the secure link, and I'll review them. Thank you for reaching out, Mr. Pettigrew. It's good to get right back to work after a vacation. It helps fend off any sort of stagnation."

Mr. Pettigrew chuckled, and the men said their goodbyes.

Winston set his phone down on the table, shook his head and got to his feet.

"Ghosts," he murmured in the stillness of the room and chuckled as he brought his dishes to the sink.

Chapter 9
Mason, New Hampshire

Winston looked like a native New Englander. Of that, he had no doubt. He had purchased his attire from a Goodwill in Hudson, New Hampshire. While the boots were a size too big, it didn't matter. He wasn't fighting in the clothes. All Winston needed to do was deposit one of three items that had been sent to him.

He currently sat in his Ford pickup, a "Hunt NH" bumper sticker on the left side of the rear bumper and a "Fish NH" bumper sticker on the right. He even had a gun rack on his rear window, but there was no weapon in it. Winston didn't want too much attention.

He glanced down at the map, took a sip of the sharp, bitter corner store coffee he had picked up half an hour earlier, and looked at the section where Mr. Pettigrew wanted the item placed.

On a side road, half a mile from a newly developed neighborhood, stood a covered bridge. Mr. Pettigrew wanted the item placed somewhere on the bridge. Anywhere, so long as it wouldn't be found.

Winston didn't think that would be much of an issue. He'd been watching the road the bridge was on for two days, and he had the traffic pattern down. Between twelve thirty and one in the afternoon appeared to be the optimal time, which meant he would do exactly that in twenty minutes.

As he sat and waited for the time to pass, he took out the gloves Mr. Pettigrew had mailed along with the three items. The gloves were essential for handling the objects, or so Mr. Pettigrew had instructed.

Winston doubted that was true, but it was part of the job. He always completed the job according to the customer's wants, and Mr.

Pettigrew was a good customer. While he hadn't ever hired him for a killing before, there had been plenty of other jobs Winston had completed. Sabotage, breaking and entering, falsification of evidence, and many more.

So, if Mr. Pettigrew wanted him to wear the gloves, Winston would wear the gloves.

They were, according to the instructions, laced with iron. The metal would directly interact with the ghosts, no mention as to how, and the metal would disrupt the ability of the ghosts to manifest. Again, no mention as to how.

No, Winston wasn't any sort of believer.

However, he did believe in getting paid and doing the job he was hired for.

He pulled on the heavy gloves and picked up the first item. He hadn't seen it, and he didn't intend to. The item had come in a maroon, crushed velvet bag, and Winston would put the bag on the bridge. From there, the ghost could do its thing, whatever that might be.

With the bag held loosely in his hand, Winston exited his truck and walked toward the covered bridge.

✳ ✳ ✳

Bert Dupont picked up his cell phone and looked at the text from his grandson.

Tylenol?

Bert muttered under his breath, and he typed in his slow, ponderous way, "Upstairs. My bathroom. In the medicine cabinet."

With a shake of his head, Bert put the cell phone down on the seat of his cruiser. His grandson had gotten himself beat down at the Milford VFW for picking a fight again. Bert understood why. There were plenty of men who came from war, and there was usually something wrong. Usually, it worked out, it had for him, and he hoped it would work out for Bert Junior sooner rather than later.

Still, it was hard being in the house with him at times. Junior would come home from work and sulk, and Bert would just need to up and leave. When Sheriff Bowman had called him and asked him to pick up the night shift for Analise, Bert had been more than happy to oblige.

Leaving his cell phone in the cruiser, Bert climbed out and stretched. It was nigh on ten o'clock and nature was calling. Around him, he heard the rumbling of the Willow Brook, and Bert picked his way down to the wooded slope toward the bank of the brook. He knew he couldn't make it to the Front Street Market, where the night clerk would let him use the restroom. Bert just couldn't trust his bladder anymore. One of the problems of getting old.

When he reached the bank, Bert shivered as a bit of cold air washed over him. He looked for a good tree to huckle up close to in order to relieve himself, and he caught a glimpse of movement.

"Officer?" a woman asked. Her voice was soft and came from the darkness ahead of him.

"It's Deputy, Miss," Bert replied. "Can I help you? What are you doing down by the water?"

"Enjoying the sound of the brook," the unseen woman replied. "It's been a while."

Something felt off about her, and Bert fought the urge to reach for his weapon. "Miss, could you do me a favor and step out into the light? I'm a little worried you might not be okay."

"Oh, I'm fine, officer," she replied, her voice coming a little closer.

"Not an officer, Miss," Bert repeated. "It's unusual to have someone out this late and down by the brook."

"You are still law enforcement."

"I am," he confirmed. "I'm a sworn member of the law enforcement community. Please, for your own well-being, Miss, step into the light."

She did so, and Bert's breath caught in his throat for a moment.

The woman reminded him of the screen vixens of the forties and the fifties, starlets who had dominated the silver screen. She was beautiful, clad in a black evening gown and wearing just the right amount of makeup. Her hair was perfectly coifed, and she carried a small black clutch.

"You see, officer," the woman smiled, taking another step closer. "Everything is fine. My name is Gretchen, by the way."

Bert cleared his throat, and when he went to respond, he stopped.

He could see through her. Right through her.

For the first time, Bert realized he couldn't hear any animals, not even any insects.

She smiled at him and took another step forward, one that he matched as he took a step back.

"I like police officers," she told him, her voice husky. "So very much. I knew quite a few before I died. I liked making them feel like heroes, but I don't suppose I can do that anymore. Not with any success. Do you know, they were always happy when they died?"

Bert's blood thundered in his ears, drowning out the sound of the brook, and her voice dropped down to a whisper.

"They were happy because I had given them the greatest gift, and they died in the afterglow of it," she sighed. "That's not possible now. Not with me being dead. I tried it a few times over the years, and it just doesn't work. Now, I'm only left with making myself feel good, so I'll take what I can get. You understand, don't you, officer?"

"Deputy Sheriff," Bert whispered and then tried to run from the dead woman.

Her laughter rang out across the brook, and her hand clamped around his throat.

CHAPTER 10
ADVERTISING

Robert closed the door as he walked out of the room, and Ezra scanned the printed pages the man had brought in. Most of the information was old, at least to Ezra. He had received a good deal of it in real-time due to a significant amount of bribes he had placed and systems he had purchased access to.

A reserve deputy sheriff had died in the town of Mason, New Hampshire, down by a small brook. There were no details yet, but Ezra had crime scene photos of the body, and it looked as though the man had been strangled. The marks on the neck were consistent not only with manual strangulation but with extreme frostbite as well.

It was now time to send out some advertising pieces. Material to catch Stan Owen's attention and to get the man to leave Ezra well enough alone.

Ezra had spent a significant amount of time on the advertising, working alone on each. He had no desire for either Robert or Abigail to become any more involved than they already were. He understood that his attempt at gallantry was more than likely too little too late, but he needed to try. Over the years, both his assistants had proven to be far more loyal than any others he had employed.

Ezra brought up the first advertisement.

Adam's friend, it's time to leave well enough alone. More of my friends are going to say the same thing to you. If you agree that the relationship is done, and it's time to move on, respond to PO Box 2015 in our town. Once you respond in the affirmative, my friends will stop.

Ezra read it through several more times, making certain the piece was clear. He had two others with similar language ready to go. When he was satisfied everything was right with them, he sent them through a false email and payment system. The papers would publish them in a few days, plenty of time for the first of the ghosts to wreak some havoc in Mason.

Ezra looked at the burner phone Robert had purchased for him earlier in the day. It was charged and ready, with only two numbers programmed into it. Ezra hadn't bothered with a voice modulator of any sort. He wouldn't need it, and he suspected it would only make the people he would call suspect it was some sort of prank.

Ezra wanted them to know it was about as far from a prank as they could get.

Picking up the phone, he pressed the first programmed number.

It rang twice before it was answered, and a woman said, "Diner."

"Good morning, I would like to leave a message for Stan Owens, if I may."

"Sure," the woman replied, chuckling. "I'll pass it along when he's in for dinner. Alright, go ahead."

"Please, tell Stan that he should check the papers. There's a message for him in the personals. It concerns some mutual friends of ours in Mason," Ezra stated. He could hear the scratch of a pen on paper over the phone.

"Okay, mysterious," she laughed. "Anything else?"

"No, you've been quite helpful," Ezra assured her and then bid her farewell.

He ended the call, took a deep breath, and called the second number.

"Good morning, this is Marilyn," the woman on the other end answered.

"Good morning," Ezra replied. "Might I leave a message with you for Stan Owens?"

"Certainly."

Ezra repeated the statement he had given to the waitress at the diner, and when he finished, he waited for Marilyn to respond.

"Sir, I don't know who you are," she said, her voice cold and hard. "I don't believe you know Stanley. I'm going to offer you a bit of advice, and you may do with it as you will. Leave him be. In the end, you will be pleased you did so."

"Madam," Ezra started.

She cut him off. "You know the story of the man who grabbed the tiger by the tail? He didn't dare hang on, and he didn't dare let go. I will deliver your message, but you are reaching for the tail, sir."

Before he could reply, Marilyn hung up.

Ezra continued to hold the phone to his ear for a heartbeat longer, then he closed it and set it on the desk. A shiver danced along his spine, and he shook it away quickly.

Stanley Owens was a thorn in his side.

Nothing more, and nothing less.

CHAPTER 11

MESSAGE RECEIVED

Stan walked along the sidewalk, head bent down slightly and his hands clasped behind his back. The old sodium lights of the street lamps flickered and cast their weak light upon him, lengthening and shortening his shadow as he moved.

He had received the message from Ezra Pettigrew at the diner. Stan knew it could be no other person. Confirmation of this had come when he had returned home and found another call had been made to Marilyn's. She had not been blind as to what the significance of the call was. Marilyn didn't know the specifics, but she understood it didn't bode well.

Stan had then gone to the library, and with the permission of the librarian, who had been in the act of closing up, he had quickly checked the advertisements.

The local papers all carried the same message in a variety of themes.

Ezra Pettigrew wanted Stan to stop looking for him.

It didn't bother Stan that the man had somehow learned of it. Nor did it bother him that Pettigrew had left messages.

What bothered him was the threat, and the fact that the threat was now a reality.

Bert Dupont was dead.

No one was saying why, but Sheriff Bowman had called and asked Stan to come down to the station. He had offered to send along a cruiser, but Stan had told him no. He wanted the time to think about Bert's death and the messages. If Sherrif Bowman wanted him at the station, then it meant there was something more to Bert's death. The man might have been murdered, and not by any living entity.

Sheriff Bowman knew about Stan's work. He had, in fact, assisted him at times, although not directly against any ghosts. He had brought Stan to those who needed help.

In a short time, Stan arrived at the station, passed by the pair of cruisers parked out front, and entered the building. Sheriff Bowman and Deputy Virgil Cummings stood at the front, leaning against the desk.

"I could have picked you up, Stan," Virgil said.

"I am well aware of your ability to drive, Deputy Cummings," Stan responded. "A quiet walk allows me to think, and that is what I needed."

"Come on into my office," Sheriff Bowman motioned. "I'll show you what we have. Bert's body has been transferred to Davis Funeral Home in Nashua."

"Do you have photographs for me to review, then?" Stan asked, following the sheriff.

Bowman nodded. "I do."

They entered the office, and Stan closed the door behind them before taking a seat across from the sheriff's desk. As always, Stan was impressed with the orderliness of the room. The sheriff followed the old maxim of a place for everything and everything in its place.

When the sheriff sat down, he picked up a set of photos and passed it over the desk to Stan, who accepted them and settled back to review each one.

They were simple shots.

Bert Dupont, still trim in his uniform, lay on his back. His eyes held the unmistakable glaze of death, and he looked as though he had collapsed close to the brook's bank. Black, necrotic flesh curled up and out of the collar of his shirt. The next photo was a close-up of the neck, the shirt pulled back. Stan could make out a rough hand shape on each side of Bert's neck, and the damage to the flesh was severe.

"Small hands," Sheriff Bowman stated. "If I had to guess, I'd say a woman or a helluva small man."

Stan nodded his agreement. "Why was he there?"

"Bert's bladder wasn't as strong as it used to be," the sheriff sighed. "He never did cut down on his coffee, though. I suspect he was just making a quick pit stop. Have you ever seen a ghost down there?"

"No," Stan answered, shaking his head. "That does not mean anything, though, Sheriff. They could have been left there, or they could have just awakened. Any number of events could have occurred which would have resulted in the arrival of a ghost."

"Will you hunt it for me?" Bowman asked, his voice low.

"Of course, I would be happy to," Stan told him. "It is a large area. I do not know if the ghost will be located centrally there or if this is at the extreme range of their influence. Either way, it may take some time to locate them."

"I know," Bowman said. "Going out tonight would be pointless."

"Agreed. I will begin at dawn."

The sheriff looked at him with surprise. "Well, I appreciate that, Stan. I know how you're keeping an eye on Adam."

"I am," Stan answered. "But I cannot help him. I can, however, help the town, and that is what I will do."

"What do you need from me?" Bowman asked.

"A ride home later," Stan replied. "Now, if I might, I would like to review the images and the map. Perhaps a ride in the morning."

Bowman smiled. "Thank you, Stan."

"You are quite welcome."

"Do you want a cup of tea?" Bowman asked.

Stan hesitated, then nodded. "Yes, please."

Stan did not specify what he liked. Bowman, like Marilyn, knew exactly how he took his tea.

CHAPTER 12

HOW MANY DEATHS?

At 97 years old, Mortimer Dunkel had seen a great deal of life. He had experienced the joy of two wives, both of whom cancer had claimed, and he had suffered the sorrow of burying all three of his children. Four grandchildren, too, and one great-grandchild. His progeny alone occupied an entire row in the small section that still remained unoccupied at Mason Cemetery. There was room for him, of course, as well as whichever two of his relations died next. If they wanted.

Mortimer paused, leaned on his cane and looked up the length of Concord Street toward the Mull Sisters' Bridge. The town had refurbished the bridge when the new developments had been built, and it was a sound investment as far as Mortimer was concerned. It had taken them too damned long, though.

He fumbled around in his coat pocket, found his hunting pipe and flipped open the windcap with one gnarled thumb. From the same pocket, he extracted a kitchen match and popped it with the nail of the same thumb. The matchhead burst into flame and he touched it to the tobacco prepacked into the pipe bowl.

Mortimer shook out the matchhead and stood for a moment, drawing in slow, steady breaths until the tobacco caught. When it did, he tossed away the match, slipped the windcap closed and continued along Concord Street. His cane thumped, a reminder of old injuries come back to haunt him, and he couldn't help but grin. If his grandchildren or great-grandchildren could see him smoking and walking at dusk, they'd be more than a trifle upset.

Mortimer snorted at the idea. They thought he was some fragile bit of glass, an old relic ready to crumble at the slightest breeze.

They forgot he had survived Parris Island in 1943 and fought the Japanese in the Pacific. They forgot how he'd been at Chosin Reservoir in 1950 and fought the Chinese. They forgot about Vietnam in 1965, when he was there sweating in the jungles and teaching men how to fight. And they forgot about his decades as a Boston police officer.

Mortimer never forgot. And when he got home to his small apartment in the center of Mason, he'd pour himself a double shot of whiskey. One for himself and one for his dead. He would do it until the day he died.

Which, he readily admitted to himself, would be sooner rather than later.

Mortimer reached the bridge, and the thump of his cane took on an echoing quality as he started across the wooden walkway. He wasn't halfway across when he felt a cold bit of air.

Mortimer stopped, frowned, and slipped his free hand into his pocket.

"And who are you?" a woman asked from a few feet ahead.

Mortimer could make out her form and nothing more.

"Just an old man out for a walk," he replied, and in the depths of his pocket, he managed to take hold of his lucky charm. The smooth edges of it offered comfort. "Who might you be?"

"How about your name first?" she replied, and she moved out a little to where he could see her better despite the flickering of the light above them.

Mortimer's breath caught in his throat, and not because he could see through the woman.

He recognized her.

She didn't know him, though, and for that, he was thankful.

"Well," Mortimer smiled, "Gretchen, I think we'll hold off mine."

Her eyes widened, and the dead woman took a step back. Mortimer wanted to take a moment and check his own pulse to see if he was having a heart attack, or maybe a stroke, but he didn't. He had managed dealings with the dead in the past, but that had been back in 1991, shortly before he had retired.

"How do you know my name?" she hissed at him.

Still holding onto his lucky charm, Mortimer took his hand out of his pocket, removed the pipe stem from his mouth and replied, "I was a police officer in Boston. Actually, just becoming a detective when you were going about your business."

She shook her head. "No. You don't know who I am. You only think you do."

"Gretchen Fortier. You hunted police in some of the smaller towns in the area. Groton, Tyngsborough, Pepperell, and a few others. It took a bit to find out who you were. You know you're dead?"

"Yes," she snarled. "What's your name?!"

Mortimer felt an old calm slip over him. He had experienced it in combat, and every time, he had a suspect in the box, waiting for interrogation.

It was the calm of control.

"You may call me 'Detective', Ms. Fortier," Mortimer answered. "I was never one of your 'white knights'."

The dead woman stiffened.

"We found your journals," Mortimer continued, pausing a moment later to take a long pull off his pipe. He exhaled a stream of smoke around the pipestem. "I thought it was a bit foolish of you to write down what you did. If we had caught you while you were alive, those journals would have been a brilliant bit of evidence."

"You had no right," she started, moving forward.

"I had every right," Mortimer snapped, the authority in his voice stopping her once more. "I don't know why you're here, Ms. Fortier, but I suspect you're responsible for the death of Bert Dupont the other night."

"What will you do about that, hmm, Detective?" she hissed.

Mortimer smiled. "I don't know. But I do know you're going to leave travelers on this bridge alone. It doesn't need a troll."

"I'll kill you," she told him, her voice suddenly flat.

"That's a good possibility," he nodded. "Until then, I'm going to turn around and walk home. You've ruined my evening, I'm sorry to say. I don't know if you have the ability to leave this place, but I would suggest you do. This isn't a safe spot for you. Not safe at all."

Still clutching his good luck charm in his hand, Mortimer turned around and started toward home. He could feel her watching him, felt the cold, burning hatred in her. The good luck charm pressed into his flesh, the long-dulled edges of the coffin nail familiar and comforting. He had carried it through his wars and his entire time as a policeman and detective. Twice he had used it to fend off the dead, remembering the old sergeant from Maine who had taught him how.

Without speeding up and resisting the urge to see if she still stood on the bridge, Mortimer focused on getting home and making a phone call.

Stan Owens needed to know about the dead killer on the bridge.

✳ ✳ ✳

Two days had passed since the death of Reserve Deputy Sheriff Bert Dupont.

Two days and nothing had been sent to the PO box. Not a single item. Ezra had sent the assassin to check twice. Not even a spiteful note or something threatening. It was as though the message had never been received.

Ezra felt certain that wasn't the case.

The assassin knew exactly what Stan Owens looked like and where he lived.

The phone rang, and Ezra answered it.

"Yes?"

"Mr. Pettigrew?"

"Hello, Winston," Ezra greeted. "Have you had any luck?"

"No," Winston replied, grumbling. "I have a question, though. When he eventually learns about the bridge, do you think he'll find this object?"

"It depends," Ezra answered. "I passed on a warning to the dead, and we will see whether Gretchen takes me seriously or not. If she does, she will hide, and this should give us a significant amount of time to build up a stronger force against him. If she does not, well, then we will lose a valuable resource."

"Mr. Pettigrew," Winston began, "I can rough him up a little bit, if that's what you need."

"No," Ezra replied. "I don't believe that will be necessary. At least, not yet. I won't dismiss it out of hand, however. Have there been any other attacks? Have you spoken with Gretchen?"

Winston paused before he answered. "No, I haven't spoken with her. As far as I know, there haven't been any other attacks, either. This is a tight-lipped community. Even though I look like a New Englander, I'm not one of their New Englanders, if that makes sense."

"It does," Ezra stated. "We're all tribal when it comes right down to it. Well, regardless of whether someone has been injured or not, keep me abreast of the situation, please."

"Will do, sir."

Once Winston had hung up, Ezra put his phone down and shifted in his seat to face the laptop. He had hoped for something to be in the papers. Perhaps a local burglary, a beating. Preferably another death, but Gretchen was essentially a free agent.

She would do what she wanted when she wanted.

CHAPTER 13

THE PHONE CALL

Stan lay on his bed, facing the ceiling with his hand on his belly, the fingers interlocked. He stared at the pressed tin, following the lines and the patterns with his eyes, tracking them on their inevitable return to the center. From the center of the room hung a small light with an opaque glass shade.

A sliver of daylight slipped in around the edges of the shade over the room's single, narrow window

He thought about the phone call from Mortimer and the information the old man had passed along. A killer on the bridge.

Stan did not doubt Mortimer. He had no reason to. Mortimer had always told the truth, even when lying would have benefited him more. And, what was of greater importance, Stan had helped to rescue Mortimer's second wife, whose name he could never remember.

That was a difficult memory for Stan to process, one he did not care for. He had only been home for a few months after his release from Walter Reed Hospital, and the dead had come for Mortimer's wife.

She had disturbed them.

Unbeknownst to either Mortimer or his wife, their apartment building had been built upon the edge of a much older farm. Mortimer's wife had a green thumb, and she went into the cleared portion of the lot behind the building and planted roses.

For some reason, Stan had never learned the act of planting roses, and only roses had enraged the dead.

The ghosts of three women and one man played havoc whenever

she went outside, and it simply became too much for the woman to bear. She felt herself trapped in the house, and her hair had started falling out. She couldn't sleep for fear of the dead, and so Mortimer had reached out to him.

Stan had negotiated with the dead and explained the misunderstanding.

Explained what might happen if they continued to bother Mortimer's wife.

The negotiations had ended successfully for all sides concerned. Mortimer's wife would no longer be harassed whenever she set foot out of the building. The dead would have sunflowers and day lilies instead of roses.

Stan's ability to negotiate with the dead had shown him that he could do such a thing.

The phone call from Mortimer had reminded him of that.

Stan had gone to the bridge twice each day since the call, but he hadn't had any luck in finding any sort of trigger item or in being attacked.

After dinner, he would try again.

With a sigh, Stan closed his eyes and allowed his thoughts to drift and old memories to rise.

✻ ✻ ✻

Two weeks.

Two weeks since he had returned from Walter Reed hospital and found himself in Mason, New Hampshire.

Nothing seemed to have changed despite the years between his initial leaving and his return. The diner still stood in the same place, Main Street was still in need of fresh paint along the asphalt, and the men who sat outside the convenience store on the corner of Main and Atticus remained. They smoked their cigarettes and pipes, chewed their tobacco and drank apple jack, the homebrewed alcohol they all favored, out of battered Thermos.

No one recognized Stan, and he appreciated that.

He was heavier than when he had left, an inch taller, too. His hair had grayed prematurely while in the hospital, and he was still conquering a limp that was a reminder of his injury. Stan also wore a three-piece suit, one picked up in a Washington, DC thrift shop.

He looked nothing like the young, wicked man who had left years earlier.

But that man remained, and Stan struggled against himself.

He paused in front of the public library and saw the first ghost in town since his arrival. He had seen others, of course. More than a few in Washington, and the ghost of an elderly man at the Manchester Airport. That dead man had stood outside the main entrance to the terminal, holding a brown suitcase and waiting for a taxi that would never come.

Stan focused on the ghost by the library.

A young woman, perhaps in her twenties, had a look of confusion on her face. From what he could guess, she had died sometime in the 1940s or '50s. When she turned to look at the library, he saw the massive hole in the back of her head.

Stan winced, clasped his hands behind his back and moved down the street. He would return later, when he was settled in, to see if he might help her. He needed to go home to the place where he had suffered for years.

But not yet.

First, he wanted to walk some more. The slow pace of Mason was a welcoming change to the manic nature of Walter Reed and Washington. Even Manchester Airport had been too much for him.

He walked for another five minutes, then turned left onto Olive Street, only to come upon a sheriff's cruiser parked in front of a house, the backyard of which was dug up. Yellow caution tape was strung around the entire property, and the sheriff leaned against the roof of his cruiser, fingers drumming on the metal.

In silence, Stan walked over to him and stood by the car. He knew the house. Kathryn Adams had lived there alone after her husband had passed when Stan was still a boy. She had been a quiet woman, worked in the factory, and didn't socialize.

The sheriff glanced over at him.

"New in town?" the man asked.

Stan shook his head.

The sheriff frowned. "I haven't seen you before."

"I have been gone," Stan answered, shifting his attention from Kathryn's house to the sheriff. "I have only just returned."

"Where've you been?"

"In the Army," Stan replied. "Iraq. Then Walter Reed."

"Welcome back, then," the sheriff stated, and he offered his hand. "I am Sheriff Bowman."

"Paul Bowman? It's Stan Owens," he said as he shook the sheriff's hand. "I see you have made sheriff now."

"Well, I'll be damned. I did not recognize you. My apologies," Sheriff Bowman replied. "Good to have you back, Stan. Hope you don't get into too much trouble this time."

Stan nodded before changing tack. "What happened to Mrs. Adams?"

Sheriff Bowman shifted his attention fully to Stan. "If you're just getting back, you won't know the local gossip."

"I arrived just this morning," Stan stated. "You are the first person with whom I have spoken."

The sheriff hesitated, then said, "Mrs. Adams died at home, and we found her body yesterday after a welfare check. She was religious about getting her mail, and after a day of not bringing it in, the mailman asked for her to be checked on. Looks like she had died of natural causes in bed. But she seemed to be expecting it. There was a letter on her bed table, confessing to burying a body in the backyard. Well, I asked the State Police to bring in a dog, just to satisfy my own curiosity, and sure enough, the dog found one."

Stan thought of the ghost at the library and frowned. "The remains of a young woman? Executed by a single shot to the head, more than likely through the mouth? It was a high-caliber pistol, was it not? There was not much left of the back of her skull."

The sheriff looked at him, blinked and shook his head. "What?"

Stan nodded. "She died sometime in the forties or fifties, correct?"

"If you weren't as young as you are," Sheriff Bowman began, his voice low, "I'd think you did it. How in the hell do you know all this? How can you know? Did your granduncle have something to do with it?"

"I saw her this morning," Stan replied.

"Who?"

"The victim," Stan informed him. "She was standing in front of the library, looking confused. Her clothing reminded me of movies like *Casablanca*. When she turned around, I saw the hole in the back of her head. Only those who have recently been disturbed look confused."

"What in the hell are you talking about?"

"I see ghosts, Sheriff Bowman," Stan answered, looking back at the house. "I have since I was wounded in Iraq."

✷ ✷ ✷

A knock on the door interrupted his reminiscing.

"Tea in five minutes, Stan," Marilyn said, and then her steps retreated down the hall.

Stan got out of bed, made certain his suit and accouterments were in order, and then left his room.

Tea was not to be missed.

Chapter 14
Gary Burroughs

All Gary Burroughs wanted to be was a police officer.

He'd been dreaming of it ever since he'd seen one arrest a guy on Main Street in Nashua, and that had been thirty years ago, when Gary was six.

Gary couldn't be a police officer.

Gary didn't quite understand how things worked.

He knew how they were supposed to work, he just couldn't understand why. If someone asked him a math question, Gary laughed. He laughed not because he was afraid, but because the numbers never stood still. Even when someone would speak a number, the numbers slipped away. Sometimes, when doctors were asking him questions, they had to use pictures of animals and fruit because he couldn't look at numbers. He couldn't look at words.

Something just didn't work.

They had sent Gary to a couple of schools, but it wasn't just the words and numbers that weren't sticking. Rules didn't hang around, either. Nothing did, not really. And Gary was okay with that.

He was okay with it because he watched a lot of television shows.

A real lot.

He watched the old Sherlock Holmes movies, and he watched the new ones, too. Gary knew every line from movies like *The Big Sleep* and *The Maltese Falcon*. He watched every episode of *Law & Order*, *Hill Street Blues* and every possible police show his family could find for him.

Gary Burroughs might not remember how to add or subtract or what a capital letter was, but he knew how to dust for finger prints and how to read a suspect their Miranda Rights. He knew bad guys went to jail, and all police were good guys.

Just look at Sheriff Bowman.

It was why Gary was at the covered bridge where Mr. Dupont had died. Something hadn't been right. Gary had heard his dad and uncle talking about it. Something was weird. Mr. Dupont had been strangled, and there was frostbite on his neck.

Nobody knew why.

And Gary knew he could figure it out. Not because he was smarter than everyone; he knew he sure wasn't.

But he did know more about police work, and he wouldn't even go and bother Sheriff Bowman. Well, not until he found out who killed Mr. Dupont.

Gary needed to get down to the brook's edge, which was where Mr. Dupont had been found.

Gary needed to see the scene of the crime, to look for evidence that might have been missed, and, according to the best shows and movies, he needed to "get into the killer's mind".

"I can do it," he told himself and looked at the trail cutting through the brush down to the brook.

Gary didn't like the brush. It's where ticks hid. Ticks liked to bite, to burrow. He had watched his dad take them off Molly, their spaniel, more than once, and Gary hated the way their legs moved and how they were bloated with Molly's blood.

They were vampires, and Gary was sure they would turn him into a tick if they bit him enough.

He hadn't mentioned that to anyone because he knew it was true. He could, as his grandma said, feel it in his bones.

Gary took his plastic deputy sheriff's badge, courtesy of Sheriff Bowman, out of his pants pocket and clipped it to his breast pocket. From his back pocket, he removed his folded baseball cap that had a gold sheriff's badge on it and slipped the hat onto his head.

He took a deep breath and stepped off the road and onto the trail. A shiver of fear raced through him, and Gary clenched his teeth as he forced himself down through the brush.

It took him almost five minutes to reach the brook, but he reached it, and when he did, he paused to take in several long, gulping breaths. His heart hammered against his chest, and he looked around, trying to calm himself, looking for anything he could fix his attention on.

His gaze swept under the bridge and stopped.

Gary thought he saw someone.

For a moment, a fresh fear flickered through his conscience, but he shook it away.

He was a deputy sheriff. Sheriff Bowman had said so, and Gary didn't need to be afraid. He had the power of the law on his side. Justice and righteousness would guide him.

Gary cleared his voice and called out, "Who's under the bridge?"

No one answered, but he saw a shadow of movement near the farthest trestle on the right.

Gary straightened up and raised his voice. "My name is Deputy Sheriff Gary Burroughs, and the law says you have to talk to me."

"Deputy Sheriff?" a woman asked from under the bridge.

Gary nodded and tried to remember what the strong police officers sounded like in the shows. "Yes, Ma'am, I am Deputy Sheriff Gary Burroughs."

She hesitated, then came out a little more, just so he could make out her face. Something seemed off about her, but he couldn't quite put his finger on it. A smile spread across her face.

"Deputy sheriff sounds like an awful big position for a young man like yourself."

Gary gave a solemn nod, hooked his thumbs through the belt loops above his pockets and said, "Yes, Ma'am, it is. I have been specially appointed by Sheriff Bowman to be his special deputy. It is very important."

"Well, Deputy Sheriff Burroughs," the woman began, "I am very glad you're here. I think I may have a problem, and I'm not really certain how to solve it."

He frowned. "I am working on a very important case right now, Ma'am."

"If it's about that terrible murder that happened the other night, then we're talking about the same thing."

Gary blinked in surprise. "Really, Ma'am?"

"Oh yes, Deputy Sheriff Burroughs," she nodded, and for the first time, Gary realized she was a pretty woman, although there was something a little off about her face.

"You see," she continued, "I don't have anywhere to live, and so, I was here, hiding and trying to keep warm, when I heard a car stop."

She coughed suddenly and doubled over. She looked at him, smiled weakly and asked, "Could you come over here, Deputy Sheriff Burroughs? I'm afraid I don't feel well. It might be sleeping out in the cold and under the bridge, or it might be the beating my husband gave me before I left."

"A beating?" Gary asked, horrified.

She nodded. "It would be so much easier for me to talk if you could come here. We could sit in the light, where it's warm."

"Yes, Ma'am," Gary nodded, and he crossed the brook, wading up to his thighs and ignoring the violent cold water. She sat down on a large stone close to the trestle as he drew near and smiled when he clambered up onto the other stones.

His body shook from the cold, and she motioned him forward.

"Come here, Deputy Sheriff Burroughs," she told him and patted the stone.

Shivering and shaking, Gary did so. He shifted so he could look at her as she lifted her arms and draped them around his shoulders.

"You're very brave," she whispered, and as she leaned in closer, Gary understood why her face had looked strange.

He could see through it.

CHAPTER 15

WHERE?

Bert Dupont had been murdered.

Gary Burroughs, a child in a man's body, had been murdered as well.

Both were left with the marks of frostbite and strangulation around their necks. Both at the brook.

Bert had been covering a shift for the sheriff's department. Gary had been "working" as a deputy sheriff. The man-child had loved law enforcement, and the plastic star Sheriff Bowman had given him lay on the man's desk.

Stan stood at the brook, the morning light shining brilliant and beautiful on the water. Like Gary, he had gone to the crime scene.

Unlike Gary, Stan knew—and had known –he was looking for a ghost.

But the ghost knew to avoid him.

Stan walked along the brook's bank to where Bert's corpse had been found. Once there, he stopped and turned, looking at the bridge. Gary's body had been located underneath it, his clothes waterlogged and with frostbite around his throat.

"Where are you?" Stan asked, clasping his hands behind his back. He asked the question in a low voice.

Only the sound of the brook could be heard. The air, absent of bird and animal sounds, hung around him.

"I find it curious," Stan continued, walking toward the bridge. "That you have killed two, but only here. Why is that? I suspect your object is here."

Something shimmered beneath the bridge, but Stan did not look at it. He waited.

"I have a theory," Stan stated. "Since both of those you killed were acting as law enforcement officers, you seem to favor them. Is this why you have not struck? Am I not your preferred target?"

Stan came to a stop only a few feet from the underside of the bridge. In his peripheral vision, he saw the ghost.

She was comely, with a mixture of wickedness and innocence flitting across her face. Her clothes placed her time of death around the 1940s, perhaps even the early 1950s. She watched him with a small smile as though enjoying his questing.

"Do you know you killed a boy last night?" Stan asked, and he saw a quick glimpse of confusion on her face.

"He looked like a man. His voice even had the pitch of a man's," Stan continued. "Yet he was not. Gary Burroughs was a boy trapped in a man's body. His status as a 'deputy sheriff' had been given to him by the sheriff because Gary loved the police. He was, in the parlance of your time, a simpleton."

Stan shifted his position and looked at the woman.

"You murdered two people," Stan told her as the ghost looked at him with undisguised shock. "One of them was a volunteer law enforcement officer. The other, a man-child. What is your name?"

"Gretchen," the dead woman answered. She appeared uncomfortable. "He wasn't a boy."

"But he was, Gretchen," Stan stated. "He could tell you the name of every leading policeman in a television show. He could not tell you the names of the actors. Gary would be able to quote you, chapter and verse, the statutes and laws of a dozen different states, but only if he heard them on a show. He could neither add nor subtract, he could neither read nor write. But, he was a good boy, and you killed him as surely as you killed Bert Dupont. Your killings cannot continue. Not only because it is wrong, but you cannot attack children."

"He didn't look like a child!" Gretchen snapped, stepping forward, her passage through the water causing a thin film of ice to form upon it. "How could I know?!"

Stan looked at her. "You could not know. He did not sound like a child. Especially when he spoke about justice and righteousness, two of his favorite subjects. There are others in town similar to Gary. Not the same, of course, but the outskirts of Mason are a place where many find peace. Where people come to protect their families."

"I didn't know," she whispered.

"Of course, you did not. But you know now, Gretchen. What will you do?"

She looked at him, confused. "What do you mean?"

"You may come with me," Stan told her. "I will take you to a place where I keep other ghosts. Or, if you resist, I will remove you from the bridge and bring you to your end."

Gretchen opened her mouth, then closed it. She looked to where Gary's body had been discovered.

"Where do you keep other ghosts?" she asked, her voice soft.

"In a room, inside lead boxes," he answered.

"Do they ever come out?"

"Occasionally," Stan informed her. "I do check on them, allow them to stretch if they wish."

"Stretch," she murmured.

A silence rose between them, and Stan waited. He knew he could not rush her, not without risking a peaceful end to the confrontation.

"Follow me," she said after a moment, straightening up. "I will show you where my object is, and we will go to where you keep the dead."

Winston lowered his birding glasses and shook his head. From his position in a copse of trees up the road from the covered bridge, he had seen Stan Owens enter and then recover the haunted object. And Winston could have sworn Owens was talking to someone.

It could have been a phone call, or it just might be that the man talked to himself. He seemed like the kind of guy who would.

Winston couldn't think of any other reason for it.

With a sigh, he took out his cell phone and sent a quick text to Mr. Pettigrew.

First object was found by Owens and removed. Next step?

CHAPTER 16

AT THE FLEAMARKET

Stan stood in a patch of sunlight and looked out over the Hollis Fleamarket. A trickle of sweat worked its way down the center of his back, and for a moment, he allowed himself to feel its path. Then, he ignored the sensation and focused on the task before him.

He needed iron.

Quite a bit of it if he was to protect Mason.

Stan left the patch of sunlight and walked into the first long aisle tucked beneath old and weathered pines. He moved at a steady pace, eyes scanning each sectioned-off area, seeking skeleton keys and nails, hinges and chains, anything made from iron. He had called around the scrapyards in the state, but he had discovered they would be a last resort. The price for iron was high at the scrapyards, and it would be difficult to move. A great deal of it came in the form of old fencing, panels removed from homes and cemeteries under expansion.

Stan did not wish to pay for the "architectural" element of the fencing.

He needed the protection iron offered against the dead, and a line of keys around a neighborhood would suffice, as well as a piece of fencing.

And Mason needed the protection.

He had spoken with Gretchen Fortier, and she was with him. He held no judgment against her, for he knew that in some, killing was nothing more than a reflex or an itch to scratch. Stan was well-familiar with violence and those who wallowed in it.

He had not asked her why she killed or why she hunted law

enforcement officers. Instead, Stan had questioned her about her presence in Mason. Had someone dropped her accidentally? Had she recently been unearthed?

The answer to both questions had been an unequivocal no.

Someone had brought her to Mason. Someone she didn't know. But she could tell him who had purchased her, and that statement alone had caused Stan to raise his eyebrow.

Someone had purchased her item, a broken doll's head. A gentleman with the first name Ezra. This man had spoken with her and two others, telling them they would be needed to commit violence in Mason, including death if needed. Gretchen had found it necessary.

As for the person who had brought her to Mason, and who had placed her on the bridge, that she didn't know. That man had not introduced himself nor spoken to her. He had set her down and moved on. She had seen him several times before but ignored him.

Stan paused before an older woman sitting in a battered folding chair. She wore a wide-brim gardening hat and was reading a ragged paperback of *Something Wicked This Way Comes* by Ray Bradbury. Around the woman's broad feet, a variety of items were strewn about a black and red checkered picnic blanket.

She looked over her bright blue reading glasses, placed a thick finger into the paperback to mark her page and asked, "Looking for something in particular?"

"Keys," Stan replied. "Any sort of ironwork, if you will."

"Iron?"

"Yes."

"I don't know about iron," she started, nodding her head toward a large plastic tub off to the left. "Plenty of metal in there. My husband, I do believe, was part crow. That man couldn't look at anything with a shine to it and not bring the thing home."

She narrowed her eyes. "You've a might nice suit on, and that metal's plenty dirty. You sure you want to dig around in there?"

"I am," Stan stated, and he moved toward the tub. "That is an excellent book."

"Hmm? Oh, yeah, it is," she chuckled, holding it up. "I found it down in my husband's workroom when he passed. Lots of books like this. Science fiction, horror, fantasy. Honestly, my daughter and I were surprised."

Stan unbuttoned his suit jacket and sat down in front of the tub. "Why were you surprised?"

"Two reasons," she said. "First, we didn't think he liked to read books like this. Only time we saw him reading upstairs was when he had his nose in a book on mechanics. Second, we felt sure there'd be some of those, you know, gentlemen's books about women with loose morals."

Stan nodded. "Yes. It is often surprising what we find when someone has passed away."

"It most certainly is," she agreed. The woman looked at him a moment before asking, "You sure you okay with getting dirty, mister?"

"Yes," Stan told her, and he forced himself to give her what he hoped was a reassuring smile. "I am quite fine with getting dirty. There are worse things for me to worry over."

She sighed, opened her book and nodded. "You got that right, mister."

The woman turned the page, and Stan began to sort through the keys.

CHAPTER 17

DISBELIEF

Ezra shook his head.

"I'm sorry, sir," Robert apologized. "I wish I had some news for you."

"I know," Ezra muttered. Then, he cleared his throat and added, "I'm not upset with you, Robert. Merely frustrated with the current situation."

"Completely understood, sir," Robert said.

"Well, let me get in touch with my contact," Ezra sighed. "You and Abigail may leave for the evening. I should be fine until tomorrow."

Robert nodded his head before he left the room.

Once the door closed, Ezra turned his attention to the laptop. He quickly accessed his accounts and searched through them again for any notification that there might be a message from Stan Owens.

There was nothing.

But there should be.

As far as Ezra knew, there had been at least two attacks, if not more. Those two had resulted in fatalities, and while Ezra didn't want death to be the final outcome of every encounter between a townsperson and Gretchen, he didn't mind all that much, either.

He took out the burner phone he had purchased for communication between himself and Winston and saw that the phone had finally finished updating. It took several more minutes for the rest of them to come online, but when it did, Ezra saw a single text message from Winston.

Ezra's heart skipped a beat, and he thumbed it open with growing excitement.

But a simple statement waited for him.

Gretchen had betrayed him, it seemed, and she had gone off with Stan Owens. While Winston hadn't said as much, Ezra knew it. Owens could see the dead, and somehow, he had convinced the dead woman to work with him.

"That's unacceptable," Ezra muttered to himself. "Who does she think she is? She's there to kill and frighten, nothing else."

He shook his head.

Ezra wanted to know *why* the dead woman had led Owens to her object. Was it voluntary? Did Owens have some sort of power over the ghost that Ezra didn't know of? Could there be such a thing?

He knew he was unfamiliar with the paranormal. In fact, he was nothing more than a novice at best.

He fought down the urge to search for some sort of explanation. That sort of meandering through the internet could wait until the task at hand was finished. And it was the task at hand that mattered.

That, and nothing else.

Ezra didn't text Winston. He called him.

The man answered before the first ring could finish.

"I was wondering when you were going to call," Winston stated.

"Technological issues," Ezra snorted. "I would have called sooner if I had known. As it was, my phone wasn't working properly."

"Understood. So, you saw that the first pigeon has left her coop. What about the other two?"

"Release the second," Ezra answered.

"Just the second?"

"Yes," Ezra sighed. "Put her close to downtown so she can see the sights."

"Sure," Winston chuckled. "I have to get a new library card anyway."

The call ended, and Ezra put the phone down on the desk.

With any luck, Shirley would be more active and stronger than Gretchen.

CHAPTER 18
DEPLOYED

Winston brought the second item into the center of Mason.

He had no appreciation for New England. None whatsoever.

Maybe, he thought, it might be better in a city, but Mason was nothing more than a point on a map as far as he was concerned. The closest thing to excitement, from what he had gathered, was the opening of bow season.

With a sigh, Winston got out of his truck, left it unlocked—the way the rest of the hicks in town did—and carried Shirley's item in his pocket. He entered the post office and glanced up at the lobby lights as they flickered.

He thought about how the lights should be fixed. The postal service didn't need a lawsuit from some New England hillbilly who suffered an epileptic seizure because of the sporadic lighting. That line of thought brought him to the question as to whether an epileptic in New England would even know if they had such a thing, considering how foolish they all seemed to be.

Winston pushed the thoughts away and focused on the job at hand. He waved hello to the bored postal worker as she glanced up from her phone, and the woman waved back, flashing him a perfunctory smile before returning to her electronic addiction.

Winston walked to the PO Boxes, found the one rented for him by Mr. Pettigrew and opened it. He kept his gloves on as he took Shirley's item out of his pocket and placed it in. Then, he settled a small cardboard box over the item, securing it in place with a bit of tape to make sure no one removed or questioned the walnut shell he had placed there.

As he closed and locked the door, Winston wondered why the dead woman was supposedly attached to a walnut shell. He also wondered who she had killed. Mr. Pettigrew hadn't informed him, and Winston hadn't thought to ask. Now, with boredom weighing down on him, he found himself curious as to the ghost's past.

He chuckled as he left the post office. He still found it difficult to accept the reality of ghosts, but there had been two corpses at the bridge, and there was no denying that.

When he reached his truck and climbed back in, he wondered when Shirley might strike.

✳ ✳ ✳

Arty Derr hummed and limped along the alley that ran between the post office and the old Mason Savings and Loans building. He couldn't remember what the building was used for now, but the Savings and Loans had gone bust in 2008, and the last business he recalled being in there was some sort of thrift shop.

But that had been in 2010, right before he went up to Concord for armed robbery and attempted assault.

He paused beside a trio of metal trash barrels and balanced precariously on his bad foot before giving the closest barrel a quick kick. The force of the blow caused the barrels to rattle against one another, and Arty was pleased to see half a dozen rats scurry out and race down the alley into the shadows.

Arty didn't like rats. Never had.

Leaning over the first of the battered barrels, Arty started picking through the trash. He looked for anything he could trade or sell, anything he could eat or drink. Life was tough when you were down, but Arty had been lower than this before, and he knew he could climb back up and out.

It was staying up and out that was tricky for him.

The first bag he removed had nothing but real trash in it. Used tissues, women's hygiene products and some shredded paper. The second bag in the barrel revealed a couple of finds. First, there was an unopened box of store-brand Fruit Loops—Frootie Oohs with Great Fruit Flavor (2% real fruit juice used!)—that was only a month past its sell-by date. Arty paused long enough to put the find in his rucksack. It was, as the saying went, a dog-eat-dog world, and he knew someone would steal it from him if he left it on the ground.

Plus, a cop might accuse him of littering and send him back for a violation of his parole. Arty didn't want to go back to prison, at least not yet. He wanted to enjoy the nice weather before it got any colder.

He shifted his attention back to the trash and then froze.

A woman stood not five feet from him on the right. He paused, smiled and straightened up.

"I'm sorry," he said by way of greeting. "Is this your trash?"

The woman, who wore a yellow pantsuit and glittering platform shoes, shook her head, and her light brown ringlets of hair bounced as she did so. She smiled at him, and that simple expression caused his stomach to knot.

Something was wrong with her. He could see it.

And he could see through her.

Arty clearly saw a Ford pickup parked on the other side of the street, the driver sitting in it and looking down the alley.

Arty felt certain the man was watching the entire scenario unfold.

When the stranger in the truck lifted up a phone and aimed it at him, Arty knew he was right.

But it didn't matter.

The see-through woman walked toward him.

✹ ✹ ✹

Winston watched through the phone's video app as he recorded the interaction between the homeless man in the alley and the ghost Winston could only assume was Shirley.

Part of him felt mildly disconcerted with the translucent nature of the woman, although the sight of the yellow pants suit reminded him of pictures of his aunt from the seventies. That memory vanished when Shirley stepped forward.

The homeless man turned to run, and Shirley grabbed him by the back of the head.

Not the hair. Not the hood of the sweatshirt he wore.

She grabbed him by the head.

The man twisted around in her grasp, and Winston saw the pure terror on the man's face. When the victim opened his mouth to scream, Shirley used her free hand to close it. She pushed up on his jaw and cut off any noise.

She must have spoken to the homeless man. His eyes widened, and he tried to free himself by swinging first at her, then at her arm. His hands passed through her form, and a happy laugh rolled out from the alley. When Winston heard it, he shuddered, and the camera trembled in his hand.

*** *** ***

Arty dropped to his knees as the dead woman pushed him, her fingers burning through his skin and bone. She tilted his head back a fraction of an inch at a time until he was staring up at him.

"Were you ever married?" she asked, her voice gentle as she took her hand away from his chin.

"No," he whispered.

"Good," the dead woman replied. "You have that going for you. If you had, well, this wouldn't end quite as well as it will."

She squeezed his head, and a whimpered moan escaped his lips.

"I don't have a lot of use for men," the ghost continued. "Even less for men who have gotten married. Marriage usually means they have found some poor woman and tricked her into a life of servitude. My first three husbands thought that. They learned."

"Please," Arty begged.

The dead woman nodded. "We'll be done in a moment. I promise. I want you to understand I do enjoy this. I won't deny it. But I do it for a reason. I'm protecting a woman from you. Don't bother arguing with me, it'll just make me mad. I want you to understand the reason, though. Do you?"

Arty wept and nodded as best he could.

The homeless man flailed about, and Winston lowered his camera. Without looking back down the alley, he started the engine, shifted into drive and pulled out into the street. He was lucky no one was coming, but even if there had been, he wouldn't have let it stop him.

He wasn't sure how Shirley was killing the homeless man, only that it looked far too painful.

Winston didn't know what sort of thrill she might get out of it, but he didn't like it. Kills should be quick and clean. No reason to drag it out.

At the next corner, he took a right and used the back roads to take him out of town. He would send the video to Mr. Pettigrew later in the day. He also hoped Stan Owens would get the message. While he didn't want to see anyone else die the way the homeless man did, he also wanted to make sure the job got done.

And if that meant watching a dozen strangers get murdered, then so be it.

CHAPTER 19

AT THE POST OFFICE

Stan overheard Marcy complaining at the post office.

"The lights," she told Doug Gall, an electrician's apprentice. "They won't stop flickering."

Doug nodded with polite concern. "Have they brought anyone in yet to take a look at them?"

Marcy snorted. "Like that's going to happen."

"I'm sorry, Marcy," Doug sighed, gathering up his mail. "Seems like you're having a rough time of it."

"More annoying than anything else," Marcy sighed, then chuckled. "Anyway, sorry to talk your ear off this morning."

"Not a problem," Doug grinned. "You're a welcome distraction, Marcy. See you in a couple of days."

Stan watched the two wave goodbye to each other, and then he turned his attention back to his PO Box. As he did, he saw frost had formed over the glass front of the PO Box a few rows over from his own.

Frost and flickering lights.

Stan lowered his hand and waited. A moment later, the lights flickered above him.

He closed his eyes and remembered the last two days. Sheriff Bowman had informed him about the body of a transient man found in the alley between the post office and the old savings and loans. Later that evening, Mr. Toby Kraus, of Manchester, New Hampshire, had suffered a fatal heart attack while driving along Main Street. There was a single spot of frostbite on the man's chest, over his heart.

Both deaths had been marked with frostbite. Both had been easily within the radius of the post office. Was it as simple as that?

Stan opened his eyes and looked once more at the PO Box with the frosted glass.

Yes, it was as simple as that.

Stan turned and walked to the counter, where Marcy checked her phone. The younger woman looked up as he came to a stop, and a broad smile spread across her face.

"Stan!" she exclaimed, putting her phone away. "How are you?"

"I am doing well, Marcy, how are you?"

She grinned. "I'm alive, Stan. That means I'm great."

"I am quite glad you are," Stan told her.

"Well, I should hope so," she laughed. "Especially seeing as how you're the reason I'm still alive. Every time I walk by the cemetery, I think of you."

"Do you walk by it often?" Stan asked, surprised.

"Every day," Marcy nodded. "It's a good reminder of where I've been and what was done for me. I can never thank you enough, Stan. I hope you know it."

"I do, Marcy," Stan answered. "I have a favor to ask of you, if I might?"

"Anything."

"I heard you speak of the lights." He looked toward the overhead lights, which flickered again as he spoke. "I believe I know the reason why you are having electrical issues."

She frowned. "It's not the wiring, is it?"

"It is not."

"What do you need?" Marcy asked.

"I need access to one of the PO Boxes, and I need the post office empty, at least for a short time."

Marcy nodded. "Give me five minutes to get the place cleared out, and then it's yours until you need it."

It took Marcy less than five minutes to empty the building. Once she told the three other employees that Stan needed it, there was nothing to talk about.

She unlocked the frosted PO Box, then she gave Stan a quick hug before she left the building, securing it behind her.

Stan went to the frosted PO Box and opened it. Inside stood a small package and no other mail. Ice crystals on the metal interior shimmered in the light, and Stan reached in. The cardboard packaging moved to one side and revealed a split walnut shell.

"What are you doing?"

Stan turned around and saw a dead woman standing a dozen or so feet from him. She wore a yellow pantsuit and a pair of heels that looked more appropriate for the dance floor than anywhere else. Her thin face, framed by carefully prepared ringlets of hair, showed a barely contained rage.

"I am preparing to remove your item from this PO Box," he told her.

The dead woman stepped forward. "No."

He extracted a small, lead-lined box from his suitcoat's pocket. "Yes."

"Are you married?" she asked, moving toward him again.

"No," Stan answered, and he plucked the walnut out of the PO Box.

The ghost threw herself at him, hitting him with enough force to knock him backward before she vanished. Stan stumbled, slammed into the floor, and grunted as he rolled onto his belly, quickly getting back to his feet. He still held the walnut and the lead-lined container.

The dead woman reappeared a few feet away, an expression of shock on her face.

"Why did that hurt?" she demanded.

"Iron," Stan told her and dropped the walnut into the box. The dead woman lunged at him again, but Stan closed the lid and secured it, the woman disappearing instantly as he did so.

He remained motionless for a moment, forcing the pain in his back and head away. His skull throbbed where it had struck the marble floor, and his lower back ached. He would need some sort of painkiller for the evening, but he would speak with Marilyn about it first. She knew best what he might require to sleep comfortably.

Even as he walked toward the front entrance, the pain settled in, and Stan hoped it would not be too difficult for him to walk home.

He didn't want to order a cab or accept a ride.

He needed to think about who had the audacity to place the ghost in the post office, and he needed to discover what it was the dead woman might know.

And that meant a trip out to the warehouse. He would not question her in the Cellar Hole. That risked discovery. At least in the warehouse, he could ask his questions, and when he was finished, he could be completely finished.

He knew how to destroy the dead, and that was exactly what he was going to do with this one.

CHAPTER 20

FOR YOUR VIEWING PLEASURE

Ezra didn't think he would enjoy such a video. Nor did he think he would enjoy it as much as he did. A small part of himself found it worrisome that he derived pleasure from watching a man die. Especially since it was a man he didn't know, someone he had nothing against and who had done nothing to him.

But it was only a small part, and one that was easily silenced.

He replayed the video Winston had sent him, and he watched Shirley kill the homeless man. She had done it deftly and in an intriguing fashion.

His phone rang, and when Ezra saw it was Winston, he answered it.

"Winston!" he greeted the man cheerfully. "I have received your video. I must thank you again. While I regret the death of the man, I know it's a necessity. I am hoping Stan Owens will see the same thing."

"You're welcome, Mr. Pettigrew," Winston answered. "Speaking of the death, I'd like to mention another death that I'm certain Shirley was responsible for. Not necessarily fully, but most assuredly the majority."

"What happened?" Ezra asked.

"There was a car accident," Winston replied. "From what I was able to learn, there was a bit of frostbite above his heart."

"Two in one day?" Ezra chuckled. "That's good news, Winston, thank you."

"Well, don't thank me, yet," Winston warned.

"What's wrong?"

"Shirley was taken." Winston's statement hung in the air.

"How is that even possible? Who took her?"

"Stan Owens, from what I've been able to gather," Winston answered.

Ezra frowned. "Tell me what happened."

As Winston spoke, telling him about the closing of the post office, Ezra's frown deepened.

"And you checked the PO Box?" Ezra interrupted.

"Yes, Mr. Pettigrew," Winston responded. "Only a few minutes before I called."

"Did anyone see you?" Ezra asked.

"No, sir," Winston answered. "I was in and out, and the staff seemed more concerned with congratulating one employee for allowing Owens to do what he did."

Ezra muttered a curse, but that was all.

"Mr. Pettigrew," Winston began.

"Yes?"

"Who is Owens?" Winston asked. "I've learned a lot about him and this town, but not too much about him, personally. Why is the entire town on this guy's side? Shouldn't there be some people who don't like him?"

"I'm not certain," Ezra admitted. "That doesn't matter, though. I want you to put out the last object. I need Owens brought to heel sooner rather than later."

"Yes, sir," Winston said. "I'll find a good spot, and we'll take it from there."

The call ended, and Ezra set the phone down.

If this final ghost didn't bring Owens under some sort of control, Ezra would be forced to find more ghosts.

Which meant a call to Morrigan and the securing of more ghosts.

Which meant, of course, more money.

✳ ✳ ✳

The warehouse stood on a dead end in a Merrimack, New Hampshire, business district that had seen better days.

How Stan's granduncle had come to own it, Stan could only imagine.

And he didn't want to.

Stan had been dropped off at the opening of the business district by an Uber driver who hadn't asked questions, which Stan appreciated. The walk from the entrance to the warehouse had taken the better part of an hour, and he had appreciated that as well.

It had given him time to think. Time to consider the advertisements in the papers. The messages left for him at the diner and at Marilyn's.

Ezra Pettigrew was responsible for multiple deaths, and he was going to pay the butcher's bill when Stan presented it to him.

A slight frown creased his brow as he thought about finding Pettigrew and how he had not heard from Shane Ryan. He hoped Shane would have some sort of answer for him soon.

And Stan knew he would need to answer Pettigrew soon. Not in the way the man wanted, of course, but in a way he would understand and remember. Stan's granduncle had taught him a wide variety of methods for making lasting impressions.

Stan let himself into the warehouse, shut off the silent alarm, turned on the dim sodium lights that hung from the ceiling, and walked toward the center. He had decided, after Bert Dupont Senior's death, to create a killing floor. Somewhere far removed from Mason where he might dispose of a ghost without a risk of interruptions. He did not want anyone from town to see what he could do to the dead.

In the center of the warehouse, which stood equally distant from each door and where the roof was tallest, Stan had constructed a secure square. Lead, salt and iron were woven in a thick pattern, creating a ten-foot by ten-foot space with a single black square in the center. Above the square stood Stan's own version of the proverbial Sword of Damocles. A block of steel weighing one hundred pounds hung above the plate. Controlled by a simple pulley and a belaying pin attached to the nearest support beam, it would crush whatever item Stan placed on the plate.

Stan stepped into the square, took the lead box out of his pocket, opened it and shook the walnut shell out into his hand. Cold and vile in his palm, he held it long enough to set it in the center of the plate. Once finished, he stepped out and walked over to the support beam where the belaying pin waited. Beside the beam was a battered office chair he had found in the warehouse office.

Stan unbuttoned his suitcoat and sat down. He interlaced his fingers on his lap and waited.

An hour passed before the dead woman ventured out of her object.

She paced the square, a look of fury on her face as she tried to find a way out.

Stan watched as she did this for some time and nodded in approval as she attempted to leap over the barrier.

Finally, she took a step back and crossed her arms over her chest.

"What do you want?" she demanded.

"Nothing."

She blinked. "What?"

Stan didn't respond.

"Did you really just say you don't want anything?" she asked.

"Yes."

"Then why am I here?!" she snapped.

"Because this is where I am going to destroy you," Stan answered.

A look of surprise flashed across her face, and then she laughed and shook her head. "For a moment, I almost believed you."

"That moment should have lasted longer," he replied. "I am telling the truth."

She laughed even harder at his statement, and when she finished, she grinned at him. "You're funny."

"I was not trying to be." Stan leaned forward. "What is your name?"

"None of your business."

"That is true," Stan admitted. "Mine is Stan. I am going to destroy you in just a minute. I wanted to express my displeasure at the murders you committed."

"Express all you want," she sneered. "I'll kill more just as soon as I'm out of here."

"Which is why you are not leaving," Stan reminded her. "Please, you must remember that I am going to destroy you in a minute."

"You can't," the dead woman laughed. "Look at you. I bet you're wearing an iron bracelet or some such nonsense. It's the only explanation for what happened before. But this little wall can't hold me for long. I'll break out, and I'll find you. Simple as that. Then, when I do, I'm going to take my time with you. Really, take my time. I want you to know that."

"That is an interesting statement," Stan remarked. "Especially considering you are the one imprisoned. Have you ever heard the story of the Sword of Damocles?"

She uttered an expletive, and Stan shrugged.

"It is a simple story. It is about a king named Damocles, and there is a sword above his throne. The sword, suspended by a thin thread, serves as a reminder that he may be killed at any time," Stan explained. "I have my own, but it is more akin to a guillotine than a sword. Call it a flight of fancy, if you will."

"And where is your little flight of fancy?" she laughed.

"Where was the sword in the story?"

The dead woman looked up and saw the weight suspended above

the platform where her item rested. Stan watched as her eyes followed the passage of the cable supporting the weight to where it was held in place by the belaying pin.

"What's that going to do to me?" she asked. "I'm dead."

"With the crushing of your object," Stan informed her, "you will be destroyed."

She shook her head. "It can't be destroyed. I possess it."

"An interesting theory, but it is fallible. Your object is real and, therefore, subject to the rules of physics. When I drop the weight, the weight will crush the walnut shell. The walnut shell cannot bear the weight nor the impact of it," Stan continued. "The weight and the force of the impact will result in the physical destruction of the walnut shell. This destruction will destroy your object's ability to keep you within it, and thus, you will be destroyed."

The dead woman looked up at the weight again, then back to Stan. For the first time, he saw concern on her face.

"You won't do it," she stated.

"I will."

"If you were going to, you would have done it before now. Talking to me about it is akin to torture," she snapped. "Good guys don't torture people. Living or dead."

"What gave you the idea that I am a good guy?" Stan asked.

The dead woman's eyes widened as Stan reached out and pulled the belaying pin.

CHAPTER 21

AT THE HOSPITAL

It was after visiting ours, but the hospital staff didn't mind. Stan had overheard them before, talking about how he wasn't a problem, and that was good. He did not wish to be a problem for them. They took care of Adam, and that was all he wanted. The young man had suffered much, and they still did not know if he would recover from his injuries.

Stan hoped Adam did.

In the relative stillness of the room, Stan cleared his throat and spoke in a low tone.

"I have captured one ghost and destroyed another," Stan stated. "I was surprised one surrendered, but I am pleased. She did offer up pertinent information regarding the man who put you here. A man I look forward to seeing soon. The second ghost, however, was neither helpful nor was she repentant for the crimes committed. She was a brute, and so I destroyed her."

Stan looked down at the tiled floor beneath his shoes.

"I still relish these acts of violence," he told his unconscious friend. "I do not know that I ever spoke with you about my childhood or the horror that accompanied it. I do know that most people react poorly to such information, and it is difficult for me to gauge how others will react. How will I be seen? I know that I am tainted by my granduncle's wickedness."

He cleared his throat. "People are being threatened in town, Adam. People are being killed. It is the same man who caused the turmoil at the factory. The man responsible for Kenny's death. I am hunting him now. Slowly. Soon, I hope, I will be able to repay him for the misery he has caused. I find myself fantasizing about it, thinking about different ways to kill him. Then, I must remind myself I am no longer that man. That man has been left in the past, and he must remain there. He steps forward upon occasion, but I would rather that than see him given free rein. It is not a pretty sight, and I am terrified of what I might do."

Stan sighed and looked down at his hands and the thin scars that raced across them.

"I know what I can do," he whispered. "I know what it is that I have done, Adam. Will I need to be a beast? Is that what will be required of me?"

Stan looked at his young friend, who lay motionless in the hospital bed. All he could hear were the ticking and beeping of machines and the thrum of the hospital's air system moving through the ducts above them.

"Whatever is required of me, I will do," Stan stated, getting to his feet. "It is as difficult and as simple as that."

Stan took a deep breath, released it slowly and buttoned his suit coat. "We will speak again soon, Adam."

Stan left the room and said goodbye to the ICU nurses.

He needed to get home to Marilyn's and decide what next steps to take.

✳ ✳ ✳

Revulsion surged in Winston, and he didn't bother shoving it down. He looked at the dead woman in front of him, and she, in turn, glared at him.

"I only kill infants," she repeated.

"That's not why you're here," Winston informed her. "You were told, quite clearly, what the expectations were. You agreed to them."

She raised her head slightly and looked down her nose at him. "I lied. I had assumed, wrongly it seems, that there might be a baby or two who might be in need of my special type of assistance."

"I don't care if you lied," Winston told her, disliking the fact that he was engaged in a conversation with a ghost. He struggled against the reality of it. "You are supposed to inflict damage on the townspeople."

"I'm not going to kill anyone who isn't a little babe."

Winston looked at the dead woman. She wore a style of nurse's uniform that had been popular in the 1980s, and he knew, from Mr. Pettigrew's information, that the woman had been a nurse. Other than that bit of history and the woman's name, Winston didn't know much more.

And he didn't care to, either.

"Joan," he started, "it doesn't matter if you kill the victims or not."

She frowned. "What?"

"Weren't you listening when Mr. Pettigrew explained the situation to you?"

"No," Joan answered.

Winston laughed in disbelief and shook his head. "Umm, okay. He doesn't expect you to kill anyone. In fact, it's at the point where he doesn't want anyone dead, he wants them scared. He wants you to work them up into a frenzy of fear."

She raised an eyebrow at his choice of words, but he didn't care.

Winston wanted her gone, out of his sight and out doing whatever nonsense she needed to. The more of the ghosts he saw, the less he wanted to.

They were abominations. Strong, powerful and hideous as far as he was concerned. Tools, according to Mr. Pettigrew, but they were not skillful tools. They were hammers, Winston believed, and they would smash anything in front of them.

And that was the last place Winston wanted to be.

"Fear?" the dead woman asked.

"Fear," Winston nodded.

A slow, vicious smile spread across her face. "I can do fear."

✳ ✳ ✳

Mallory Scanlan loved gardening.

She spent as much time as possible outdoors and in her backyard. Never the front. The front yard was a patio with raised beds of hardy, ornamental grasses and surrounded by a short, white picket fence. The front yard was a dangerous place to be.

Salt was thrown up by the plows in winter, and too often, a variety of sports equipment—balls, frisbees, badminton birdies, and others— ended up amongst the patio stones and grasses. The neighbors across the street from her and their half-a-dozen feral children had no sense of common decency, especially when it came to someone's yard.

And so, Mallory focused her attention on the backyard.

Long before she had purchased the property, a previous owner had installed a six-foot high chain-link fence around the roughly one acre of yard. Mallory, in turn, had first attached bamboo fencing to the chain-link, then planted rose bushes. Over almost twenty years, the roses had thrived, rising and spreading and protecting her garden from any and all intruders.

Mallory's garden stood as a testament to the beauty of nature and, whether she acknowledged it or not, to her own determination.

She had a pair of peach trees in one corner, which bore fruit in season. Her vegetables came in and provided her with fresh food for each day and canned when the fall and winter settled in. Birds, bees, butterflies and rabbits found sanctuary in her garden, and of late, she had even spotted chipmunks racing behind squirrels.

Mallory never chased the animals out. Each served its purpose, and when necessary, she moved plants. It was rarely necessary, though, as she made certain to leave out enough food for the animals to subsist upon when needed.

Nature, she knew, was a balance.

Except for the Joneses across the street. They were the exception to the rule.

The clock in the parlor struck eleven, and Mallory heard it clearly through the open window above her. She had been tending to some of the pumpkins, but the strike of the clock meant it was time for coffee and toast. She knew she needed to eat and to drink. In the past, when she was younger, she had often worked through the day without pause. A trip to her physician, however, had resulted in a slight reprimand, a reminder that she was not getting younger. Mallory had planned on ignoring the physician's advice until the woman had reminded her that if she didn't care for herself, then she would eventually be unable to care for her plants.

That, and that alone, had motivated Mallory to adjust her schedule to make the necessary changes in her life.

And so, even though the work with the pumpkins wasn't finished, she stood up and climbed the stairs into the backroom.

When she had first purchased the home, the room had served as some sort of den. She had changed that by installing shelving, grow lights and hooks. Standing in her workroom, she took off her gloves and boots, rinsed her hands in the small basin of water and dried off her hands before peeking at the onion shoots beneath the grow lights.

With a smile on her face, she left the room and traveled the well-worn path to the kitchen. She hummed a tune she had picked up from work, some pop song that played endlessly over the store speakers, and selected a dark roast coffee pod for her single-serve coffee maker. As she dropped the pod into the machine, a cold breeze swept over her and caused her teeth to rattle.

Mallory didn't like the cold. In that way, she was most assuredly like her plants.

She went to the window over the sink and peered into the backyard.

A woman in a nurse's uniform stood in the center of the yard, close to a marble bench that had cost Mallory the better part of three months' salary.

Mallory blinked.

No one should be in the garden. The only way into it was through the house. She had made sure of that.

Stunned, she hesitated a moment before stepping back, and then she stopped as the nurse vanished. Mallory rubbed her eyes, peered through the window and confirmed that the stranger had indeed disappeared.

"I wasn't out in the sun that long," Mallory murmured, then frowned as the coffee maker sputtered and whined.

Turning around, Mallory screamed.

The nurse stood behind her, an opaque presence that shouldn't have existed.

"You have quite the green thumb," the stranger stated, and her voice was filled with menace. A cruel smile crept onto her face. "Should I blacken it for you?"

"Don't touch my plants," Mallory gasped, fear sweeping over her. "Please."

"Your plants don't have a green thumb, dear," the nurse whispered, stepping closer. "But you do."

Before Mallory could move, the stranger grabbed Mallory's thumbs in her hands and squeezed.

Pain and cold, immediate and intense, shot through her and tore a ragged, terrified scream from Mallory's throat.

CHAPTER 22

ADDITIONAL INFORMATION

Stan was just finishing his meatloaf when Sheriff Bowman slid into the booth and sat across from him.

"I'm sorry to intrude, Stan," the sheriff apologized.

"It is never an intrusion, Sheriff," Stan replied. "What has happened?"

Before the sheriff could answer, Ellen stepped up, took Stan's dishes away and placed a cup of tea on the table in front of him. "Coffee, Paul?"

The sheriff nodded and smiled his thanks. Once she was a few feet away, Sheriff Bowman stated, "There's been another attack."

"Who has died?" Stan asked.

"Thankfully, no one," the sheriff answered. "But the victim is in rough shape. They took her to Southern in Nashua, and from there, she was med-flighted to Boston. They're trying to save her thumbs."

Stan frowned. "Who?"

Once more, the sheriff paused as Ellen brought a cup of coffee and several packets of creamer over.

"Mallory Scanlan," Sheriff Bowman replied. He added emptied two creamers and two packets of sugar to his coffee. The thin flatware spoon clanked around the interior of the porcelain mug for a moment, and then the sheriff set it down on a napkin. "Mallory Scanlan, who has done nothing but work on that garden of hers for thirty-four years."

Stan sipped his tea. "What did she say?"

"She said there was a woman she could see through. A woman in a nurse's uniform who wasn't really there. Mallory said the room was cold, and the stranger grabbed each of her thumbs. According to Mallory, the woman said something about green thumbs." Sheriff Bowman took a long sip of coffee. "What the hell is that about?"

"Fear," Stan answered. "They are hoping to spread fear."

"They're doing a good job," the sheriff grumbled. "Word's spreading through town that something is wrong. People are wondering what you're going to do about it."

Stan raised an eyebrow.

"I've made it known that you've done quite a bit so far," Sheriff Bowman stated. "The frequency of the attacks makes people question it, though. People know we're friends, and I suspect they think I'm just making excuses for you."

"People can be foolish at times," Stan replied. "And that is unfortunate."

"That's one way to put it."

"I am going to work on a solution to the problem of this influx of ghosts," Stan stated. "It is my hope to have the town protected, for the most part, within the next week. Unfortunately, it will take time to do so."

"I know that," Sheriff Bowman nodded. "And I know you have been working on it, Stan."

Stan finished his tea. "I will let you know how it goes, Sheriff Bowman."

"Thank you."

Stan stood, buttoned his suitcoat and left the diner.

Stan stood in the barn and looked at a map of Mason pinned to the wall. His suitcoat hung on a peg by the door, and his watch and cufflinks sat in a small, porcelain bowl on a table beneath the suitcoat.

Three hours had passed since he had spoken with the sheriff at the diner. Stan's shirt clung to his back with sweat, and his arms ached. Slowly and methodically, he flexed and relaxed his fingers. From a longer table against the wall where the map was pinned upon, he lifted a bottle of water, uncapped it, and took a long drink.

His work had been with the iron keys, heating and hammering where necessary, linking them together. He had dozens of feet bound together, and he looked at the town map. He searched for areas most easily accessed by someone with a vehicle. More importantly, someone with a vehicle who didn't want to seem out of place. This narrowed his search down to roads coming into town, for he doubted that whoever was bringing the ghosts in would risk placing an object in the center of town again. The post office ghost had been quickly resolved.

Whoever placed the ghost there to begin with would surely recognize it. He suspected the next step would be to utilize the one-mile radius of the average ghost. Placement would be on the outskirts of town, enabling ghosts to strike in places where people would not, in theory, expect an attack.

The person putting the ghosts in their positions would not be able to go into the woods outside of these areas, however. People had trail cams and saltlicks up. They were preparing for hunting season, and they were territorial when it came to the woodlands. A stranger, especially one attempting to blend in, and Stan had no doubt the person was doing exactly that, would not want to draw attention to themselves.

From the pocket of his vest, Stan removed a mechanical pencil, advanced a bit of graphite, and stepped up to the map, with careful attention to who lived where, he could isolate the most probable locations for the ghosts to be freed.

Or attempted to be freed.

Stan took another drink of his water and focused on the map.

CHAPTER 23

REFUSAL

"It wasn't entertaining."

For the first time in twenty years of being sober, Winston wanted a drink.

"What do you mean it wasn't entertaining?" he asked Joan.

The ghost shrugged, her eyes flicking to the gloves he wore, knowing full well that he was, to some extent, protected from her.

"I thought that torturing someone would be entertaining," the dead woman stated. "Trust me, I didn't think it would be fulfilling, like silencing those colicky babies, but I thought there would at least be something. But nope, not a thing. I'm not going to do it."

A pain settled behind Winston's eyes, and he pinched the bridge of his nose.

"You know," he began, "you don't have a choice in this."

She laughed. "Of course, I have a choice. What are you going to do, put me back in my box? Who cares? I don't. Either I'll come back out of it, or I won't. It's really as simple as that."

"You harmed one person. Just one," Winston said, shifting his attack. "How do you know you won't be entertained by the next one?"

"Is the next one going to be a colicky baby?" she asked.

"I don't know," he admitted.

"So, my answer is no," the dead woman shrugged. "Do whatever you want with me. I'm going to wander around and see what the world's been up to since I died."

Winston tried to speak, but Joan vanished before he could do so.

He let out a long, low hiss of frustration and then went to make a call.

✷ ✷ ✷

Ezra stared at the phone.

His call with Winston had ended only a moment before, so his anger with the situation was raw and fresh.

He didn't know how a ghost could refuse to follow through. Of course, he still had several from his first attempt in Mason, two of whom never even acknowledged his existence.

But Joan had been a killer.

A killer, he sighed, who wanted a specific type of victim. Ezra had hoped, though, she would be able to move past it. That something, somehow, would encourage her to visit violence upon anyone in Mason.

He had been wrong.

Terribly wrong.

Ezra shifted his attention from the phone to his laptop, and he opened the tab that had his financial information for ghost acquisitions. He knew without having to check it that there was plenty of funding in the accounts. Making sure, however, was a habit he intended to keep.

He picked up his phone again, dialed Morrigan's number and waited.

Like the first time he had called her, she answered immediately after the end of the third ring.

"Mr. Pettigrew," she greeted.

"Morrigan," he replied. "I hope you're well."

"I am always well, thank you. And yourself?"

"Unfortunately, I cannot say the same," he answered.

"Why is that?" she asked.

Ezra told her in short, concise language what had occurred with the last of the three ghosts, and how he seemed to be in need of additional dead.

When he finished, he asked, "Do you have more?"

"Yes, I most certainly do," she told him. "Perhaps this time I should send along three males? They might be more violent, but they will most certainly be more malleable. The stronger the female ghost, the more difficult it can be to control them. Would you like Joan destroyed?"

Ezra wanted that very much, but he didn't want to pay for it, which he suspected was next should he agree.

"No," he sighed. "We'll let her run amok. Perhaps she'll cause some sort of distraction for us. I am interested in the three males, though. I'll wire you the money immediately."

"Excellent."

"I hate to ask this," Ezra began, "but do you get a steady influx of violent ghosts?"

"It is not steady, unfortunately," she informed him. "There are not as many ghosts as people might think, and a great many of the dead only want to remain peacefully where they are. It is only a small percentage who continue to wreak havoc on the world, and they are usually only happy doing it in their narrow fields. You see this with Joan, and while this surprises me, it is not unusual. Finding these ghosts takes some effort, and thus, the reason for the high cost. More than one ghost trapper has died attempting to seize one of the dead. It is unfortunate, but it is part of the job."

"Not for the faint of heart?" Ezra asked with a chuckle.

"No," she sighed. "Not at all. I will call you soon with the details of the next shipment, Mr. Pettigrew. Until then, I suggest you keep an eye on Joan. She may become angry and attempt to lash out at whoever is dealing directly with her."

Ezra thanked her for the warning and ended the call. He put in the wire request for the funds, and then he shut his computer down. It was nearly time for him to go to the club. He had, upon his doctor's suggestion, taken up swimming. Something new and physical to help him escape the pressures of his job.

Ezra hoped it would work.

CHAPTER 24

REMINISCING

"Do you only drink tea?" Gwen asked, smiling at him.

Stan felt the heat of a blush rise up into his cheeks, and he wondered how it could be.

"No," he answered after a moment. He forced a smile, knowing it was the appropriate response.

"I'm sorry," Gwen said, her voice soft. "I forget how to interact with people when I'm not wearing my psychologist's hat."

"You have nothing to apologize for," Stan assured her. "My difficulties with interacting are my own and no one else's."

She sipped her coffee and shifted her position in her chair. Sunlight slipped in through the curtain of the coffee shop's window and highlighted her fine features.

"I don't believe that," Gwen told him, lowering her mug. "You weren't like this in grade school, Stan. This didn't happen until after your parents died."

He nodded. "That is true."

Gwen paused, then asked, "Didn't your granduncle take you in?"

He blinked. "Yes."

"That was rough." Gwen's voice was soft, her words a statement and not a question. "I don't think any of the parents really paid attention to it."

"One of the teachers did," Stan replied.

Gwen raised an eyebrow and waited for him to continue.

He hesitated only for a heartbeat.

"Do you remember Mrs. Jules?" he asked.

"Sure," Gwen nodded. "She taught 8th grade literature. We had to read *A Separate Peace*. I hated that book."

"As did I," Stan told her. "Well, Mrs. Jules appeared to notice a change in me as the year progressed, and she brought it up to Principal Monet. He, in turn, brought it to the attention of my granduncle and grandaunt."

He sipped his tea before he continued.

"What Mrs. Jules did not know, Gwen, was that Mr. Monet owed my granduncle a significant amount of money in markers. These markers showed exactly how much money Mr. Monet needed to repay my granduncle for poorly made bets on sporting events."

"Gambling debt?" she asked.

"Yes," Stan nodded. "Exactly so. Part of the way Mr. Monet kept the vig, the interest rate, low on these depts was by giving my granduncle access to the school when it was needed, and to whatever information was on file. While my granduncle would more than likely escape any sort of review from the Department of Youth and Services, he most assuredly would not have wanted any additional people looking into his business dealings. My granduncle cleared Mr. Monet's debt all for that warning. Do you remember what happened with Mrs. Jules?"

Gwen frowned in concentration, then she shook her head. "No, I don't. I think she left before the end of the school year."

"You are correct," Stan nodded. He finished his tea. "She did not complete the school year. Mrs. Jules had the misfortune of seeing my legs one day. My thighs, specifically. When my granduncle and my grandaunt beat me, it was often on the backs of my thighs. This way, the marks would not be seen, and each time I sat, it would be a reminder of what I had been punished for."

"Why were you punished?" Gwen's voice was carefully moderated, almost professional.

"In that instance?"

She nodded.

"Well, I had made the mistake of missing the target once out of fourteen times," Stan explained. "Each morning, before school, I was required to do a task. I never knew what task it would be. My granduncle, if he was home, would pull a number from a jar, and that number would correspond to a list of tasks. On that particular morning, he pulled number 98, fourteen rounds rapid fire from a Colt. Model 1911 .45. My first shot missed the center of the target by one inch and three-fifths. I received ten blows from my granduncle's leather belt for the miss."

Gwen's jaw tightened, but she remained silent.

"I went to school rather sore, and Mrs. Jules must have seen me limping. And, as I learned later, she almost walked in on me in the classroom. There was, if you remember, a long mirror in her coat closet. I had gone in before the end of lunch and lowered my pants to see how bad the marks were. The welts had risen and were still red, but they were far better than others I had received, and so I was pleased."

"But Mrs. Jules wasn't," Gwen stated.

"Indeed. Well, I am getting away from the story. When my granduncle learned of her desire to inform the authorities about the welts, he took her. He did it alone, and he brought her to a building he owned. He took the belt to her, but not just to her thighs. My granduncle beat the entire backside of her body, eventually dropping her off outside the Catholic Medical Center in Manchester. Mrs. Jules told the ER staff she didn't know what happened. My granduncle had laughed about it that night. He told me and my grandaunt that he had told Mrs. Jules that if she spoke with anyone about me or her punishment, he would personally beat each member of her family to death in front of her."

Gwen lowered her coffee mug and looked at him.

"Was this every day, Stan? The violence and the abuse?"

He considered the question for a short time, and then he nodded. "Yes. To some degree. It was only when I joined the Army that I found some sort of peace and quiet."

She let out a surprised, beautiful laugh that brought warmth up into his chest.

"I don't remember ever hearing someone describe the Army as a place of peace and quiet," Gwen grinned.

"What have you been doing, Gwen?" Stan asked. "What have you done since the end of high school?"

"I went to college," she shrugged. "I wanted to learn how to help people."

"Did you?"

She offered him a shy smile. "I did."

"Tell me, Gwen," Stan said. "How do you help people?"

Her smile broadened, and she told him.

CHAPTER 25

A LACK OF COLLABORATION

Ezra hadn't done more than glance at the specifications Morrigan had sent along with the three items. Robert had repackaged them and forwarded them to Winston. They would arrive in a day or so, plenty of time to speak with Winston and inform the man of the next steps Ezra wanted to take.

A knock on the door interrupted his thoughts and he glanced over to it, asking, "Is it important?"

"It is, sir," Robert replied, his voice slightly muffled by the door.

"Come in." Ezra leaned back in his chair and rubbed at his face. He felt tired, more so than usual. It might have been from the new swimming routine, or maybe the lack of proper rest. He didn't like to admit it, but Stan Owens had gotten under his skin.

Robert entered the room and closed the door behind him. With a nod from Ezra, the man sat down.

"What's going on, Robert?" Ezra asked.

"I was communicating with the hacker we hired, sir," Robert explained. "He informed me that out of all the names we have him checking, yours is getting a new, stronger push. The man continues to monitor, but we will need him to put up heavier walls soon. As he said, someone is bringing a bigger hammer every day. And, unfortunately, sir, he seems to be getting curious about you."

"Suggestions, Robert?"

"Hire a second hacker to begin investigating the first," Robert advised. "This should distract him, at least for a short time. By then, the situation in Mason may be resolved."

"And if not?" Ezra asked.

"You may need to hire a third to investigate and protect the original group while having someone eliminate the first hacker," Robert informed him.

Ezra chuckled. "I appreciate your practicality, Robert. Please go about setting those systems up. Start the second hacker as soon as possible, and be ready to activate the third. Thank you, Robert. I appreciate your attentiveness regarding this situation."

"Of course, sir," Robert smiled, getting to his feet. He paused and asked, "Has there been any good news out of Mason?"

Ezra snorted. "No. None at all. I'll be calling Winston in just a moment or two to see what the situation is."

"I hope there is some good news, sir," Robert said and exited the room.

As the door clicked closed behind the man, Ezra sighed.

"I hope so, too," Ezra murmured and picked up his phone.

＊＊＊

Winston answered the phone as he turned off the nightly news.

"Mr. Pettigrew," Winston greeted. "How are you?"

"I'm doing well, thank you," Mr. Pettigrew chuckled. "Still a little frustrated with Joan's refusal, but these things happen. However, I do have good news."

Winston smiled and shifted the phone to his other ear. "What news is that, sir?"

"I have a new trio of ghosts heading your way. My assistant is mailing them as we speak."

"Excellent," Winston said. "Have you any particular places in mind?"

"No, nothing leaped out at me. I was looking at a map of Mason earlier, and I just didn't see a good place in the center of town for their deployment."

"I would advise against anything in the center of town right now," Winston told him. "Stan Owens seems to know the limitations of ghosts as you've described them to me, and so if there's attack in the center of town, he'll know where to narrow his search."

"What would you suggest, then?" Mr. Pettigrew asked.

"I'd say put all three of the ghosts out at once," Winston answered. "Different spots around the border of the town. This way, they could slip into some of the edge communities. There's at least one trailer park, maybe two. And there's a small neighborhood that's definitely seen better days. The possibilities for hiding an object in the woods around the town are fantastic, plus they would allow the ghosts to really get into the town without risking quick identification from Owens."

"That sounds like an excellent plan," Mr. Pettigrew stated. "I wholeheartedly endorse it, Winston. You'll see a significant bonus for that as well. Thank you."

Winston grinned and picked up a bottle of beer. As he took a drink, Mr. Pettigrew spoke again.

"I do have one request regarding the deployment of these ghosts," Mr. Pettigrew stated.

"What's that?" Winston asked.

"I would like you to work with the ghosts."

Winston frowned, set the bottle down on the coffee table and asked, "What?"

"I would like you to work with the ghosts," Mr. Pettigrew repeated. "From what I gathered, Winston, these are men after your own heart."

"Mr. Pettigrew," Winston began, keeping tight control of his voice, "I will be happy to deploy these ghosts for you. To find the best spot for them to operate from. Should you desire me to intervene directly and kill your target or anyone else around your target, I will be happy to do that, as well. What I will not do, Mr. Pettigrew, is interact with the dead any more than I absolutely have to."

"I'd be happy to double your price," Mr. Pettigrew responded.

"The money isn't the issue," Winston told him.

"What is it then?"

"They're dead," Winston stated. "They are dead, and they should not be functioning in any capacity in this world of ours. I don't want any more involvement in this than the bare minimum that I have already."

"Winston," Mr. Pettigrew started.

"Mr. Pettigrew," Winston interrupted. "This is, as they say, a nonstarter."

A moment of silence followed, and Winston listened to his employer breathing on the other end.

"Fine," Mr. Pettigrew replied shortly, and Winston heard the forced joviality in the tone. "That's fine. Expect the package in the next day or so, Winston."

"Yes, sir."

Winston ended the call and turned the phone off before setting it down beside his beer bottle. For a short time, he did nothing more than watch the condensation form and roll down the sides of the green glass to be absorbed by the cork of the coaster.

Winston didn't work with living partners.

He surely wasn't going to work with a dead one.

CHAPTER 26

WINSTON JAMES GEOFFREY HARRINGTON III

His name smacked of entitlement, old money and good manners.

Winston was none of those.

He opened a second bottle of beer and made himself comfortable in the easy chair. He didn't bother putting the news back on. Mr. Pettigrew had, unfortunately, spoiled his mood.

Instead, Winston reflected on the current situation, which, in turn, caused him to remember his past. He wasn't afraid to look at his past. There was no reason to be afraid.

He didn't know who his father was, and he suspected his mother hadn't really known either. She had been an 'unfortunate,' and an attractive one at that. She paid for most things with the one blessing she had been given, and that was physical beauty.

Winston was not afflicted with physical attractiveness. He wasn't unattractive, either. He was a plain, average-looking man, and that had served him far better than good looks would have.

When his mother had seen him, she explained, she was horrified at how he looked. None of the nurses or doctors had bothered to tell her how babies appeared after their travel through the birth canal.

Or so she said.

Winston thought it more likely that his mother wasn't listening, and when the birth was actually occurring, the pain was too much.

She had hoped to overcome his unattractiveness by giving him a name that she believed would serve him well. And thus, he was christened Winston James Geoffrey Harrington III. There was neither a one nor a two, of course. She also informed him she didn't believe anyone in their family had ever been named Winston, James or Geoffrey. As for the last name Harrington? She had once babysat for a family named Harrington, and they had treated her well.

Harrington was the one part of his name Winston truly enjoyed.

He took a long pull off of the bottle.

His mother hadn't died well, sadly. One gentleman caller who was far from a gentleman. Winston had still been in the Army, still earning money and looking for a solid trade to transfer into when his enlistment was up.

Originally, he thought it might be good to go to a trade school. Maybe electrical or HVAC, something with a solid paycheck at the end of each week. Something that would allow his mom to stop entertaining gentlemen. The money he sent home from the Army just wasn't cutting it.

He had been looking at trade schools near his mom's apartment when he'd been informed of her death. He had been given leave to attend the funeral, which had been arranged by the members of her sewing club at St. Kathryn's, where she had gone every week.

Winston finished his second beer, stood up and went into the kitchen. He retrieved a third bottle, hesitated, then grabbed the rest of the six-pack. He carried it out to the den, sat down and set the bottles beside him. He opened the third bottle and took a drink.

He thought about the funeral. About how no one had known what his mother did for work. All they knew was that something had happened to her one night and that the police were investigating.

But they weren't investigating that hard.

For the police, it was nothing more than an accidental death. One that happened to take place in the bedroom.

Winston didn't care if it was accidental. He didn't care if it was intentional.

His mother was dead, and she had done everything she could to provide for him.

It didn't take long for him to learn that the man who had killed his mother was from Boise, Idaho, and had flown back on the morning of the funeral.

Flown back to his wife and kids.

Winston made a big deal of appearing to be drunk and stumbling into his mother's apartment. He had found the timer for the Christmas tree lights and plugged the television into it, turning it on before slipping out a back door. Dressed in some of his old clothes that still fit and with six hundred dollars he had found in his mother's underwear drawer, he traveled half an hour over the border and bought a junker for five hundred dollars. No questions asked.

The car made it to Boise, Idaho and died, which was fine with him. He could always get another.

He had wiped the car down completely before setting it on fire under an overpass, and then he had gone into the city.

It had taken him a full day to find the man who had killed his mother.

And it had taken Winston less than fifteen minutes to kill him, his wife, and their three children.

And he had made it look like a murder-suicide.

He had taken all the cash he could find and bought another car.

It took him three days from start to finish, and he had discovered the Army had already taught him a trade.

He could kill.

He could kill without compulsion.

No one in his mother's apartment building ever noticed that he hadn't, in theory, left the apartment for three days. They had heard the television turning on and off. None of them had been close enough to his mother to check on him. He had left his phone in the apartment. He would learn, later in life, that the police in Boise had thought the murder-suicide had been a result of the death of Winston's mother. An argument between husband and wife.

Winston had done twenty years in the Army, and he had mastered many weapons.

After the Army, he never worked with anyone else. There was no one else he trusted.

And if you couldn't trust the living, then you couldn't trust the dead.

Winston finished the third beer and opened the fourth.

CHAPTER 27

ASKING FOR ASSISTANCE

Stan stood in his room and finished buttoning his suit coat. Despite his restful sleep, he did not feel any better than when he had gone to bed the night before.

Exhaustion had settled into his soul, and he wasn't sure how to chase it out.

Speaking with Gwen helped him, and the thought of her brought a smile to his face. And it had helped not in a doctor-patient sort of way, but between two friends.

He shook his head, still finding it strange that she wanted to speak with him.

Stan had never been one to intermingle with the opposite gender. His teenage years had been preoccupied with survival, and his time after had been marred by violence. Violence that was either created by himself or by someone else.

Usually, though, it was a violence only a select few witnessed.

And those few were usually on the receiving end of it.

Stan exited his room and traveled down to the first floor. He went into the kitchen and found a note by the sink.

Gentlemen,
I have been called away for the evening. Please make certain you
clean up after yourselves.
Marilyn

Stan nodded to himself and turned away from the note. He would be sure to clean everything once the rest of his housemates had settled in for the evening. Some of them would forget, and one or two would intentionally not do it, but that was simply the way the world worked.

And Stan didn't mind the cleaning. It was always relaxing.

He drew a glass of water, drank it down and then washed the glass. Around him, the sounds of the house creaked and whispered. Most of the men were home from work, but they were in the midst of preparations for the evening and the weekend to follow. They had worked hard all week and, in the parlance of the land, they would play hard all weekend.

Stan would not.

He left the house and went to his workshop in the barn. Standing before the map of Mason, he looked at what he had accomplished thus far.

Of the total area he had wanted to protect, Stan had secured a quarter of it. Thin lines of red showed his progress on the map, and he hoped that by the end of the day, he would be able to extend the line. If he managed to keep the same speed as the previous days, he would have a little more than half, perhaps almost two-thirds, of the area covered.

The knowledge pleased him, although it reminded him of the danger. There hadn't been any additional attacks, but he knew it was only a matter of time before that changed.

He knew how Pettigrew would react to the destruction of his ghosts.

The man did not like to lose, and he would view the destruction of the ghosts as a loss.

He would seek to come out on top to win the competition.

Stan wouldn't let him.

But he knew he couldn't do it on his own, which was why, after placing more of the barrier, he would seek assistance.

✻ ✻ ✻

Family burial grounds dotted the town of Mason, and many of them remained hidden from the people who lived near them.

Over the decades, brush and trees, creeper vines and deadfall had covered not only the headstones but the paths to the small cemeteries as well. When the Browns sold their farm and moved in the 1960s, their family graveyard vanished within a decade. Similar stories surrounded the farms of the Lavoies, the Jones, the Hemmingways and the Coffins. The families moved or died out, and no one was left to care for the dead.

Most of the dead rested peacefully. They did not loiter about their headstones, nor did they wander the new developments of businesses near them.

But some did.

Stan knew them all.

From Mr. Coffin, who had died in 1778 from an infection after an incident with a British soldier's bayonet, to Penny Jones, who had laughed herself into an aneurysm while watching a Benny Hill rerun in 1985.

Stan knew them all because he had stopped to speak with each in turn. Even those who had no use for the living would speak with him, not out of any love for having someone to converse with—they often spoke with one another—but because he cared for the town.

He cared for both the living and the dead.

He did his best to protect it, and so the dead did their best to help him with his chosen task.

It was dusk by the time Stan climbed over the wall into the Jones' cemetery, the rumble of a tractor-trailer filling the air. He spotted Penny sitting with her back to her own headstone as she stared at a dragonfly on the other side of the wall.

She glanced at Stan, who nodded to her.

"I wish they would come in," she stated. "They don't, though."

"I am sorry," Stan offered.

Penny grinned and nodded. "I know you are, Stan, and I appreciate it. What brings you out here? It's not snowing."

She was right, of course. Stan generally paid her a visit at the first snowfall. It was an easy way for her to tell time.

"I come in search of a favor," he told her.

She got to her feet. "A favor? Now that's something different. I don't believe you've ever asked me for a favor, Stan."

"I cannot remember if I have or have not. I hope you do not mind."

"Oh, Stan," Penny laughed, "I don't think there's anything you could do that would bother me. You're a sweet kid."

"I am older than you were when you died," he reminded her.

"But I was still born before you," she said. "Don't forget."

"I will not."

"Okay, tell me what you need."

"I am afraid there are ghosts who are going to try to come into Mason," he began.

"Why?" she asked.

"In order to hurt the living."

Penny shook her head. "No. That's not going to happen. You need my help with them?"

"I might. I must speak with others first."

"What others?" Penny asked. "Like, other ghosts in town?"

"Yes."

"Don't worry about that," Penny told him. "I'll get the word out. When do you think it'll happen?"

"At any time," Stan replied. "I have begun placing iron in some of the more likely places I believe they will try to enter town, but there are other avenues where they might do so with little trouble."

"Like here?" Penny asked.

"Yes," he nodded. "Like here. I know you can visit the Lavoies from here, and they, in turn, can visit both the Coffins and Bloods."

"You'll have to speak with the Coffins," Penny told him. "They've been a bit uppity as of late. They'll listen to you, though."

"I will," Stan replied.

"Hey, Stan," Penny said as he started to leave.

"Yes?"

"Thanks."

"For what?" he asked, confused.

"For making death interesting," she winked.

Stan bowed his head and went to speak with the Coffins.

"Yeah?"

"We have found a gap," the dead man stated.

"Good," Winston grinned. "I'll check in on you all tomorrow."

The ghost vanished, and Winston returned to his truck. He needed to call Mr. Pettigrew, but that would have to wait until he was far enough away from the ghosts. Then, when he finished, he could do what he really wanted, which was to have a long shower and a cold beer, and he was looking forward to enjoying both of them.

✳ ✳ ✳

Noah Yollen built models.

It was the only hobby he had and the only one he wanted to have.

The first model he ever built was on August 2nd, 1975, when his wife emptied the bank account and left him for her cousin.

Her female cousin.

Noah had walked into Montgomery Ward's in Nashua, purchased a model of a Fokker triplane, made famous by the Red Baron during World War One, and built the plane over the next week.

It was sloppy, poorly painted and a mess to look at.

But it had helped him through the week.

Noah had been building and painting models for nearly fifty years, and he had long ago lost count of how many he had built. Some of them were in private collections, sought after by collectors of such things. He put in ridiculous details, not because he had to, but because it made him happy.

Classical music filled the house, and he looked at his newest work. It was a Vought F4U Corsair, and he was attempting to decide whether it should be preparing to take off from the flight deck of a World War Two aircraft carrier or if it should be in mid-flight providing air-ground support for advancing Marines in the Pacific.

These were important questions. He wanted to sell this model when he was finished, and some collectors wanted to add it to their aircraft carriers while others wanted to add it to their land battle dioramas.

Noah took a battered 1947 half-dollar off his modeling table. The coin was his decision-maker

He rested it on the back of his thumbnail and flipped it into the air. He followed it with his eyes as it reached its peak near the ceiling and then tumbled down to the carpeted floor. It bounced once and came down face up.

Aircraft carrier it was.

Humming, Noah turned the box over, used his thumbnail to slice open the plastic, and then removed the thin film, tossing it away into the bin beneath the modeling table. With careful, precise movements, he emptied the box. Each sprue and its attached parts were laid out on the table. He arranged them in alphabetical order, A through H, and then set the decals on a separate shelf so he wouldn't accidentally ruin them.

He had done that more than once in the past, and it was nothing he wanted to repeat. Despite his popularity with the various hobby shop owners, none of them were going to open up their shop at eight or nine, or later, in the evening should he desperately need to purchase a new model for the decals alone.

When the ritual of removing the sprues was completed, Noah stood up and went into the kitchen. He removed a small bottle of schnapps, a well-worn shot glass, and carried them into his work room. These he placed on the far right of the worktable, just out of reach even if he leaned in his chair. This would force him to stand up and stretch when it was time for a shot or two.

And thinking of stretching, Noah went into his small den. He turned on the light beside the couch and then proceeded to go through his stretching routine.

He despised it.

But if he didn't do it, sitting in his chair to build became too painful, which meant he wouldn't be able to continue building.

So, shoving his hatred for exercise aside, he commenced his workout.

It wasn't much, and it wasn't long, but by the end of fifteen minutes, he had broken out in a sweat, and his heart was thumping.

He eased himself into his wingchair, picked up a glass filled with tepid water and removed a gnat that had somehow managed to drown itself. As he took a sip, Noah frowned.

He couldn't remember when he last drank the water.

The frown slipped away.

Lunch. He had water with his sandwich and chips at lunchtime.

The frown returned.

He shouldn't have forgotten that. He didn't want to forget things.

His father had forgotten things, quite a few of them near the end, and Noah's father had only been seventy.

Noah wasn't even seventy-three. Or was it seventy-four?

Noah brought the glass to his lips and saw it was empty.

"Did I drink it all?" he muttered. He glanced around at the floor and at his sweatpants. Nothing was wet.

He brought his free hand up to his lips and his unkempt beard. His lips and beard were damp.

Noah's hand trembled as he set the glass down and refused to look at it.

"I'm not forgetting things," he said, voice shaking as he pushed himself to his feet.

As his hands let go of the arms of the wingchair, the light flickered.

Noah stared at it, and the light flickered again.

"Stop that," he told the light, and the lamp went out. There was no click, no pop of the incandescent breaking. It simply went out.

Noah looked around to make sure he was still standing by the chair, that he hadn't somehow magically crossed the room unbeknownst to himself and turned the lamp off.

He hadn't.

With a shake of his head, he left the room. He had been in the house for almost five decades. He didn't need a light to tell him how to get to his workroom.

But the workroom's lights were out, too, and that sent a spark of worry racing through him.

If he didn't have light, he wouldn't be able to work on his model.

The last time he hadn't been able to work on a model was in December of 2019 when he was afflicted with the Corona virus. That had been three weeks of pure misery. He hadn't worried about dying. He had been in the middle of a diorama of the Charge of the Light Brigade, and he had wanted to finish it. It didn't matter that the buyer was dying from Corona in the same wing of the hospital. All that mattered was finishing the model, and Noah had been more than halfway through.

As for the Vought F4U Corsair, he hadn't even begun to assemble it, and that frustrated him.

An itch started on the back of his left hand, and Noah fought the urge to scratch it. He needed to ignore it because if he didn't, if he satisfied that urge, he wouldn't stop.

Once, when the power had been out for three days in a storm, and there hadn't been enough hours in the day to work on his models, he had scratched himself raw. A scar remained from where he had received a skin graft.

A whisper caught his ear and held him still.

He didn't recognize the language, but he knew that whoever spoke it was in the house with him. Noah swallowed, and his throat emitted a surprisingly loud click, one he was certain the intruder had heard.

From the kitchen, another man spoke in the same language, and then a third called from upstairs.

Noah scratched his hand, the nails digging into the skin around the graft, his heart thudding against his thin breastbone.

He heard nothing from the house, and he should have heard everything. His home always creaked and groaned as he walked. Crossing the bedroom was a symphony of discordant howls from the century-old wood, and the kitchen floor squealed with every step.

Yet these men made no noise at all.

Noah shivered, suddenly, painfully cold.

"Don't worry," a voice said from behind him. "This will be quick."

Before Noah could speak, something wrapped around his heart and squeezed.

CHAPTER 29
CONFUSED

"Winston called while you were out, sir," Abigail told Ezra as he entered the office.

Ezra frowned. "He called the direct line?"

"He did," Abigail nodded. "He told me to tell you that it was extremely important you call him back."

"Thank you, Abigail," Ezra murmured, and he hurried into his room. He didn't bother hanging up his coat or hat. Instead, he dropped them onto his desk and picked up the cell phone. When he opened it, he saw three missed calls and three texts. Ezra dialed Winston's number, and the man answered before the first ring could finish.

"You called the main line," Ezra stated, unable to keep a disapproving tone out of his voice.

"I did," Winston replied without any hint of apology. "Something new popped up yesterday."

"It must have been after hours."

"It was," Winston confirmed. "The three new ghosts discovered something I don't think was there before."

Ezra sat down. "What?"

"Some sort of barrier."

Ezra blinked. "I'm sorry, what was that?"

"A barrier," Winston repeated. "They can't pass it in certain places. The area will look good, nice and clean, but when they try to go through it, it's like they walk into a wall."

Ezra frowned. "Have they been able to do anything?"

"Yes. They found a gap just before nightfall," Winston told him.

Ezra sighed. "Were they able to carry out at least one attack?"

"They were," Winston stated. "They told me it was one man. Older and living alone."

"Did they make it obvious?" Ezra asked. "I don't want it to seem like he died of old age. Owens needs to know it's me, and he needs to understand the seriousness of the situation. I want him to capitulate."

"Yes, sir, I know that. The ghosts stated his death was quick, but they tore him apart afterward. His body is strewn all over the apartment."

"Excellent," Ezra smiled. "Thank you for the update, Winston. I apologize for not having the phone with me."

"No need to apologize, sir," Winston chuckled. "I was taking a chance that you had the phone. I'll leave a message next time you don't answer."

"Very good," Ezra said, and they ended the call.

The ghosts had worked out, and there was a fresh death clearly attributed to the dead. At least as far as Stan Owens would be concerned. And in the end, that was all that really mattered.

Stan needed to know people were going to get hurt. People were going to die.

All Stan had to do was stop looking for Ezra. Once that was done, everyone could go back to their business.

Getting to his feet, Ezra hung up his coat and hat, opened his office door and was pleased to see Abigail preparing a cup of coffee for him.

When it came down to it, Ezra knew he had the best staff working for him.

CHAPTER 30

HOW THE PAST INFLUENCES

They sat together in the booth of the Peddler's Daughter in Nashua. Their meals were finished and Gwen had her graceful hands wrapped around an Irish coffee. Stan had a large mug of tea and a shot of whiskey beside it.

"Do you come here often?" he asked.

Gwen grinned. "Sounds like a pickup up line," she explained.

"Ah."

"And yes, I do come here often," Gwen told him. "Usually once a week. It's a good place to decompress after work and before I drive the half hour or so back into Milford. Sometimes, it's a longer drive if there's been an accident."

"When did you move to Milford?" he asked.

"Ten years ago this coming May," Gwen smiled. She took a sip of her coffee. "It's a nice little salt-box Victorian. I think I have enough money to paint it the color scheme I've always wanted."

"What colors?"

"A few different shades of purple," Gwen answered. "I had a dollhouse when I was a little girl. One my grandfather had made for me. I shouldn't say 'had.' I still have the dollhouse up in the attic. I just haven't found a good place to display it yet. Anyway, I have a dollhouse that my grandfather made and painted. I want my house to look like that."

Stan nodded. "I think that sounds wonderful, Gwen."

"What about you?" she asked. "I know you said you stay at Marilyn's, but I thought your family had a house. Didn't you get it when they passed?"

"I did," he confirmed, nodding. "I do not live in the house, although I keep it up."

She leaned back in the booth and took another drink. "If you're not going to live in it, then why keep it? Is it for sentimental reasons?"

Stan sipped his tea and considered best how to answer. To some, he told none of the truth. To others, he told some of the truth. Never had he told anyone all of the truth.

But it was time.

"I do not hold onto the home for sentimental reasons," Stan began. "It was a horrific place for me."

"You told me about the belt," Gwen murmured.

"You might consider that the least of punishments," Stan told her.

Her face paled slightly, and she took another sip of coffee before speaking. "How bad did it get, Stan?"

"I believe, at times, my granduncle read all about what is referred to now as 'advanced interrogation techniques.'" Stan looked into his mug of tea for a moment. "I was sleep deprived, denied food and water, exposed to extremes of weather, and beaten on a regular basis."

She shook her head. "What did you do wrong?"

"Wrong?" Stan sighed. "Nothing. These were everyday activities. Actions, my grandaunt and granduncle assured me, designed to strengthen me. I was taught to fight. I was taught to use knives. Everything, I learned, could be a weapon. I grew to fear my grandaunt's sewing basket. When I did fail at something, and my granduncle did not wish to use the belt, he would take out a large pincushion. I remember it clearly. Roughly eight inches in diameter, three inches tall and divided into twelve segments. At the center of each segment, around what might be considered the equator of the pincushion, was a single figurine dressed in traditional Chinese garb. My grandaunt, who had been a seamstress when she was younger, had a range of pins that varied in length and width. Some had decorative heads, others were plain steel.

All of them hurt."

Gwen set her mug on the table. "They tortured you."

Stan shrugged. "It was normal, as far as I was concerned. I did not have many friends, and I did not speak of my punishments. I was ashamed of my failures, and I did not want anyone to know."

"Your granduncle and grandaunt were monsters," she said, her voice thick with anger.

"They were," he agreed. "Eventually, I was able to turn off the pain. I never knew what would trigger a punishment, but when one commenced, I ignored it. By the time I was fifteen, my granduncle discovered this, and it pleased him."

"What?"

Stan nodded. "He was pleased I had learned how, and while he still punished me, it was not to the same degree. The physical violence served only as a reminder that I had erred."

"Why would he do that?" Gwen asked.

"I was expected to assist him with his business," Stan explained.

"What was that? Torturing people?"

"At times," Stan stated.

She looked at him, and he felt fear well up within him.

"He tortured people?" she asked, her voice low.

"Some," Stan admitted. "Usually not those he was going to kill."

"I wish you were joking," Gwen said, "but I can tell you're not."

"No," Stan sighed. "Unfortunately, I am not. My granduncle was a criminal, Gwen. He controlled a wide swath of southern New Hampshire and northern Massachusetts. He did so through violence, intimidation, and blackmail. In my youth, I was used as a tool. I delivered messages, and those were messages of violence."

"I am so sorry, Stan," Gwen whispered and reached across the table, her long fingers wrapping around his right hand. "You know you're not to blame for any of the things he made you do, right?"

"There are times when I do know and others when I do not," he admitted. "It is difficult. When my granduncle and grandaunt died, I lived alone in the house until I was old enough to join the Army without any guardian's signature."

"Did they die together?" Gwen asked. "Was it an accident?"

"They did, and it was not. My granduncle smothered my grandaunt and then died immediately from a heart attack."

She shook her head, finished her coffee and said, "What?"

"They had no love for each other at the end, and although she never threatened him, my granduncle became afraid she might talk."

"I'm surprised he didn't have you do it," Gwen stated.

"He wanted to, but there was some heavy work coming up, and he did not want me being looked at by the police for her murder. He did not like me, Gwen, but he knew how useful I was to him." Stan finished his tea. "Making myself useful was the only way I survived. He would have killed me when I was younger if I had not earned my keep. He told me that on more than one occasion. There were plenty of places he could hide my body and plenty of ways he could disassemble me to make the dispersal of my corpse easier."

"I am so sorry you went through all that, Stan," Gwen told him. "It never seemed like anything was wrong in school."

He managed a smile. "I did not want any of my teachers to be punished, not the way Mrs. Jules was. I wanted them to be safe, even those who I did not care for. They did not need to suffer because I could not take a little discipline."

"Stan," Gwen said, the sharp tone in her voice causing him to look into her eyes, "you did not receive 'a little discipline.' You were tortured and psychologically mutilated for your granduncle's purposes. That is far, far beyond a little discipline."

Her smartwatch chimed, and she frowned as she tapped on it.

"It's my mom," she informed him. "My dad's in hospice in Merrimack. You'll have to tell me about the Army another time."

"I will pay the bill," Stan told her. "You go to your family."

Gwen hesitated, then said, "I'll cover the tip then."

They both got out of the booth, and Gwen counted three fives out of her wallet. She laid them down on the table, set the edge of her mug on them to keep them in place, and then gave him a hug.

"I'm sorry for everything that happened to you, Stan." She gave him a quick kiss on the cheek. "But I'm happy you're the man you are today. We'll talk soon."

Stan felt the warmth on his cheek as she left and waved goodbye.

The warmth spread through him as he walked to the bar to settle the bill.

CHAPTER 31

INFILTRATORS

"Care for some company?" Sheriff Bowman asked.

"Sheriff," Stan replied. "I am always happy to see you."

"I know you are, Stan," the sheriff said, easing himself into the other chair in the sitting room.

"Does Marilyn know you are here?" Stan asked. "If I do not inform her, she will not forgive me."

Sheriff Bowman chuckled, an act that only accentuated the lines of stress around his eyes. "I saw her when I came in through the front. She was working on the banister. I don't know what needs to be done with it. That mahogany glows like the sun itself was hidden in the wood."

"It does," Stan agreed. "This home is a testament to her will."

Sheriff Bowman nodded.

"May I ask what brings you by?" Stan asked. "I am unfortunately certain it is not simply to pass the time."

"No, it's not," the sheriff sighed. "In fact, it's because there's been another death."

"And we are certain it is a ghost?"

"Yeah. That we are."

"Who was it?" Stan asked.

"Noah Yollen," Sheriff Bowman answered.

Stan frowned. He had not quite gotten to Noah's neighborhood, and it had cost the man his life.

"How did he die?" Stan asked.

"We're waiting for the coroner's report," the sheriff said. "But the crime scene itself shows he died before he was dismembered."

Stan looked at the sheriff. "Dismembered?"

Sheriff Bowman nodded. "He was, quite literally, torn limb from limb. Then, each limb was torn apart. He was spread all over the house. I don't think I've ever seen something quite like it."

"Marks of frostbite?" Stan asked.

"Yes. At each place where a limb was torn and separated. There are clear and distinct fingerprints. We ran them through the system, but we didn't get any hits."

Stan thought about the ads and the messages from Ezra Pettigrew, and a deep, powerful hatred churned in his stomach. "Do you know when he was killed?"

"No," Sheriff Bowman replied, shaking his head. "Seems it was close to evening, though. Noah had a new model all laid out to be assembled. I know from talking to him before that he liked to start them at night. Helped him sleep, I guess."

"I will speak with some people," Stan said, standing up. "I hope they will be able to assist me with locating the ghosts and removing them from Mason."

"Do you need a ride anywhere?" Sheriff Bowman asked, getting to his feet.

Stan shook his head. "No, thank you, Sheriff. Walking will help me think."

✳ ✳ ✳

The death and dismemberment of Noah Yollen had set a fire of rage in Stan's belly.

He remembered Noah from when his parents had died. Noah had helped Stan get to his feet, had checked to make sure he wasn't injured, and then carried him away from the scene of the accident. Not once had he allowed Stan to see what had happened to his parents. Not once had he mentioned it after the initial questioning about Stan's physical health.

Instead, Noah had stayed with him until the sheriff and the volunteer firefighters had showed up. He had stayed with Stan until the ambulance had arrived and then ridden in it with Stan into Nashua. Noah had even checked on Stan each day of the thirteen days he had been in the hospital for minor internal injuries.

Noah had brought in different models he had finished, and shown pictures of those he was considering building. He had made sure that someone had brought in Stan's favorite toy, a stormtrooper from the Star Wars movies.

Noah Yollen had been a kind man who had done nothing more than build models that made other people happy.

Someone had killed the man.

Someone had torn the man's body apart.

It had only been a week since Stan had seen Noah, and that had been at the library. Noah had been researching different paint schemes for new planes as well as unit identifiers for soldiers he was preparing to paint. They had spoken for twenty-seven minutes and made plans to have lunch at the diner within two weeks.

Stan always enjoyed Noah's company, and he had been looking forward to their dinner.

And now, the man was dead, murdered by the same man who had ordered the murder of Kenny.

Ezra Pettigrew was killing Stan's friends.

Adam was still in the hospital, and he, too, might die.

There was no guarantee the man would ever leave the ICU, even if he didn't die. He might be permanently injured.

Stan flexed his hands and forearms, feeling the minuscule pieces of steel still embedded in his flesh. At some point, he would find Ezra Pettigrew and give the man the painful death he deserved. And the sooner he could do it, the better.

Stan reached the Jones' burial ground and climbed in.

Penny came out almost immediately, an angry expression on her face, and Stan prepared himself for an onslaught of complaints about the Coffins and their unbearable dispositions.

"Strangers were here, Stan," she grumbled.

"Living?" Stan asked.

She shook her head. "Far from it. Only one of them spoke English, and he was rude, Stan. Rudest man I've ever met, and I've been next to the Coffins for almost forty years."

"What happened?"

"Well, I was with Mr. Coffin, and we were actually getting along," she admitted. "He and I were wandering that little section that overlaps between our burial plots, and along comes this group of three men. They were bloody and speaking a language I didn't get. I think it might have been Spanish, but I don't know. They were ghosts, Stan, no question about that, and they seemed like they were in a mighty fine mood."

"What did they do?" Stan asked.

"They tried to push through us," she told him. "Mr. Coffin, well, he told them no and that they were being impertinent. You know how he talks."

Stan nodded. Mr. Coffin, seeing as how he was close to three hundred years old, had a peculiar way of speaking.

"Only one of them seemed to understand what Mr. Coffin was saying, and that one said we needed to mind our own business. Our own business! Can you believe the audacity?" Penny shook her head. "Well, that was that. Before you could blink, old Mr. Coffin had that warclub of his up in the air, and he went at those dead soldiers."

"Soldiers?"

She nodded. "Didn't I say they were soldiers?"

"You did not," Stan informed her.

"Oh. Well, yeah. They were soldiers. And, as I said, they were rude.

The one who spoke English, he laughed at us, and he laughed at Mr. Coffin. That was short-lived, though," she smirked. "Evidently, he didn't think Mr. Coffin could do a thing with that old war club. Neither did I, if I'm being truthful. I always thought it was just for show. Anyway, old Mr. Coffin, he brained the closest soldier, and that one wasn't the one speaking English. Before anyone could do another thing, Mr. Coffin hit that same soldier again, and the soldier broke apart and scattered."

Penny shook her head. "I didn't know what to do. I kind of stood there for a minute, and I was about to try and throw a rock or a stick, if I could get up enough strength. But I didn't have to. Mr. Coffin hit the other soldier when the English-speaking one ducked. That soldier he hit went tumbling back, and when the English speaker punched Mr. Coffin, it bounced off him!"

"I did not realize Mr. Coffin was so strong," Stan admitted.

"Neither did I!" Penny's eyes shined bright, and she grinned at him. "Well, old Mr. Coffin ignored that punch and set about the soldier on the ground. That one tried to fade into the earth, and Mr. Coffin grabbed him by the neck and dragged him straight out into the open. A couple more punches from the English-speaking one didn't do a thing, and the whole time, Mr. Coffin was just beating the one he held with that war club. By the time that ghost vanished, the last one took off running."

"Mr. Coffin destroyed two of them?" Stan asked.

She nodded her head vigorously. "It was really great, Stan. I wish you had been there to see it."

"As do I, Penny," Stan told her. "Did he return directly to his burial ground?"

"No," she sighed. "He's out hunting the last one. You know, even though Mr. Coffin's in his fifties, and he's weird the way he talks, I think he's kind of cute. Never really noticed it until today, though."

"I would not know," Stan replied.

She smiled. "Well, anyway. Do you want to wait here?"

"I will go and wait for a spell at Mr. Coffin's," Stan stated. "If you see him first, please tell him."

"Okay," she nodded. "Um, if you see him before me, maybe ask him to stop by? I think I'd like to hear how he learned how to use that war club."

"I will most certainly do that," Stan assured her.

With a wave to the dead woman, Stan left the cemetery and headed for the Coffins' burial ground. When he finished speaking with Mr. Coffin, it would be time to answer one of Mr. Pettigrew's ads.

CHAPTER 32

RUNNING A TAB

"Did the sale go through?" Ezra asked.

Robert looked up from his tablet. "Yes, sir. I'm just reviewing the finalized paperwork now. You made a significant profit."

Ezra offered him a tired smile. "It should be. I put a lot of work into it. Quite a bit of time, actually."

"All of the profits are earmarked for the new account, correct?" Robert asked.

"Yes," Ezra nodded. "I'll essentially be running a tab with that account."

"For the ghost procurements."

"Exactly," Ezra confirmed.

Robert finished up on the tablet, shut it down, and set the device down on his lap. "Sir, if I may?"

"Yes?"

"I know I don't have all the information regarding the procurement of the ghost assets," Robert started. "But I'm wondering, is it worth this kind of investment?"

"That is a fair question," Ezra smiled. "That is also one of the reasons why you are here, Robert. You have the courage to ask difficult questions. Yes, it is worth the investment. I've been extremely satisfied with the items this dealer has provided us. She has far surpassed the original owner. I'm hopeful the last three ghosts purchased from her will deal with my Stan Owens problem. I've also discovered that the ghosts are extremely useful to have. With the right handling, of course."

"Is Winston handling them for you?"

Ezra frowned. "No, not nearly as much as I would like. They are a challenge, and there is something about them he doesn't seem to care for. I attempted to get him to take over the reins, but he didn't want that. Didn't want it to the point of breaking the contract."

Robert didn't bother to hide his surprise. "I don't think I've heard of Winston ever breaking a contract before, sir."

"I've known the man for some time, Robert, and I can assure you, I have never, not once, heard of him breaking a contract." Ezra sighed and shook his head. "I was angry at first, of course. But then, I realized it wouldn't do any good to push him. And, later, I discovered I didn't want to be known as the only man who had caused Winston to break a contract."

Robert nodded in understanding.

There was a moment of comfortable silence between the two men before it was broken by a gentle knock on the door.

"Come in, Abigail," Ezra called, and Abigail did so.

She smiled at them and said, "Mr. Pettigrew, there's a response to one of your ads."

Ezra chuckled.

"Would you like us to leave, sir?" Robert asked.

"No, no," Ezra assured him. "This should be good."

A sense of relief filled Ezra as he logged onto his computer. Stan Owens had been a terrible thorn in his side, and it had cost him an incredible amount of money to deal with the issue. Still, it was worth it. Ezra could only imagine the pitiful response he would find.

He opened his email, found the notification and followed the links to the secure response. Ezra typed in his passcode, and the smile faded from his face.

Noah Yollen was my friend.

"Who was Noah Yollen?" Ezra asked.

Robert accessed his tablet again and, within a minute, answered, "The most recent fatality in Mason, New Hampshire."

"Mr. Pettigrew," Abigail said. "Would you like an aspirin?"

Ezra was about to shake his head, but he nodded instead. "Yes, please, Abigail."

When she had left the room, Ezra looked at Robert. "Make certain those funds are available sooner rather than later."

"What's wrong, sir?" Robert asked.

"It seems the most recent fatality was another friend of Stan Owens. One close enough to cause him to respond to the ad. I think that removing him is going to require additional funding."

Robert nodded and worked silently for a few minutes.

Abigail returned without knocking, placed a glass of water and two aspirin on the desk and then left, closing the door behind her.

"Should we leave the ads up?" Robert asked.

Ezra hesitated, then nodded. "I'm going to take a chance that someone might be injured, and that an injury will cause Stan to pull his punches, so to speak. Deaths seem to make him angrier."

"Understood, sir." Robert set his tablet down. "The funds are in the account, and I have attached backups as well, sir."

"Thank you, Robert." Ezra picked up the two aspirin and swallowed them with a drink of water. "Now, if you don't mind, I have to call Winston and see if he can pull back those three ghosts we just released. I don't want another death. Not yet."

"Yes, sir."

When Robert exited the room, Ezra made the call.

✳ ✳ ✳

Winston glared at Raul, who appeared much the worse for wear.

"Where are the other two?" Winston asked, sitting on the lowered tailgate of his truck.

"Gone," the ghost answered.

Winston frowned. "Yeah, I can see they're gone. Where did they go?"

Raul glared at him and gestured toward the ground. "How many casings do you see?"

"One," Winston replied after a moment. He saw a pair of charred marks on the earth and asked, "Where are the other casings?"

"They were destroyed when their owners were destroyed," Raul snapped.

"What?"

"When a ghost is destroyed, so too the object they are attached to, and vice versa," Raul answered, his tone and expression bitter.

"Who the hell destroyed you?" Winston asked. "Was it Owens?"

Raul shook his head. "Another ghost."

Winston blinked, confused. "Are you saying ghosts can, what, kill each other?"

"Yes, though it is not common. Or rather, it never was for me," Raul said. He looked down at his own shell casing. "I did not think this would come to pass."

"What type of ghost was it?" Winston asked. "Was the guy a giant or something?"

"No," Raul answered, shaking his head. "He was my height and dressed in clothes that were very old. His English was difficult to understand as well. He had a club, and I was nothing to him."

Winston looked at the eternally bloody ghost before him. "What do you mean?"

"I watched him destroy Armand," Raul said. "Then, he caught Ernesto and dragged him up out of the earth as he sought to hide. I attacked this stranger, and my blows bounced off him. I tried to stop him, but when he destroyed Ernesto, I ran. There was nothing more I could do. I cannot face him."

Winston shook his head and then looked around. "Did you lead him here?"

"He could not have followed me," Raul replied, straightening up with pride.

Winston was about to ask how certain the dead man was when a shimmer of movement caught his attention.

Looking over Raul's shoulder, Winston saw a man approaching them.

The stranger was short, perhaps Raul's height, and he wore an antique suit with the pants bloused at the knees. White socks covered his lowered legs, and square-toed shoes adorned his feet. The man's suitcoat had tails, and his dirty blonde hair was tied back in a pigtail. In his hand, he gripped a Native American war club that could have come straight out of a movie.

Worst of it all, though, Winston could see through the man.

"Run," Winston whispered to Raul.

Raul frowned, half-turned and then let out a scream of horror.

The ghost with the club attacked with a vicious downward blow that caught Raul in the crook of his left shoulder where it met his neck, driving Raul to the ground. Winston watched as Raul began to sink into the earth, and then the ghost with the club grabbed Raul by the front of the shirt.

Raul screamed, clawing at the arm holding him, but the other ghost was unfazed.

Once more, the war club was raised high and then smashed down into Raul's head.

With two blows, Raul's head broke apart, and the shell casing exploded with a small pop reminiscent of practice grenades.

Raul vanished, and Winston sat on his tailgate, staring at the dead man across from him.

"My name is Mister Jonathan Coffin," the dead man snarled. "And I'll have no more of your dogs in my town. Mr. Owens has put us wise to your kind, sir, and he'll have you soon enough if you don't leave."

Before Winston could think to respond, the dead man turned and disappeared.

Slowly, Winston eased himself off the tailgate, closed it, and got behind the driver's wheel. He put his hand on the keys, closed his eyes, and hoped the engine would start.

It did.

CHAPTER 33
UNWANTED NEWS

Stan's conversation with Mr. Coffin had been interesting.

The dead man had informed him, without any embellishment, that the dead who had killed Noah Yollen were taken care of. Permanently. And, apparently, Mr. Coffin had run into the man who had been handling the ghosts for Mr. Pettigrew.

Stan would have liked to have spoken with that man.

He would have liked it quite a bit.

Stan looked over to Adam, who lay in the hospital bed, unmoving and unlikely to do so. Stan's heart sank at the sight of the young man, and he wondered if Adam might ever recover.

Finally, Stan stood and exited the room. It was close to two in the morning, and he would need to walk to the taxi station in order to procure a ride back to Mason.

He nodded goodnight to the nurses on duty and proceeded through the hospital toward the stairs, which he preferred to use. When he reached the door to the stairwell and entered it, he came to a stop.

A small boy sat on the landing, clad in a bathrobe and fuzzy green slippers. The boy was dead, and he looked at Stan with sadness.

"You're his friend," the boy stated.

Stan stepped fully into the landing, let the door close and took a seat on one of the steps. "Whom do you mean?"

The boy smiled. "Only my mom uses 'whom.' I mean the man in ICU. I think he said his name is Adam."

"He spoke with you?" Stan asked. "He is afraid of ghosts."

"He did speak with me," the boy nodded. "But it was not as the living to the dead. He was out of his body, at least for a short time. He is close to death."

Stan felt his shoulders sag. "He is slipping out of his body?"

"Sometimes," the boy confirmed. "We've spoken to him. We try to keep him in his body, but it's hard."

"Are there a lot of you?" Stan asked.

"Not as many as people would think," the boy said. "But more than there should be, and we speak to him. One or two tell him he can leave, but we try not to. We try to make it his own decision, as much as it can be."

"What is your name?" Stan asked.

"Toby," the boy answered. "And you're Stan. Some of the staff talk about you. They like you."

"That is kind of them."

"Some were worried you wouldn't be able to let Adam go," Toby said.

"The dead or the living?"

"Both." Toby stretched.

"I do not want him to die," Stan told him. "But I will be able to let him go. He will not be the first of my friends to have died. Unfortunately, I do not believe he will be the last. Thank you for telling me."

Stan took a deep breath, cleared his thoughts and then asked, "Have you been here for a long time, Toby?"

"In the hospital or the stairwell?" Toby asked.

"In the hospital itself," Stan clarified.

"I've been in the hospital for a long time. A really long time."

"How long?"

"I've been here since 1992," Toby told him. "It was the night of my ninth birthday. I died from a heart attack. Kind of weird, right?"

"It is strange. Did you ever learn why?" Stan asked.

Toby nodded. "They said it was, um, congenital. Is that the word?"

"Yes. That would be the word."

"Yup. I was born with it. No way anyone could have known. It made me sad, though," Toby told him.

"Why?"

"I had gotten some really awesome toys for my birthday," Toby smiled. "I never got to play with them. Some great Matchbox cars. They looked like they'd go fast."

"Matchbox cars?" Stan asked. "Would you like to have one or two?"

Toby grinned. "You could bring them here?"

"Of course."

"Do you think I could play with them? Would the people mind?" Toby asked, getting to his feet.

"I think I could find a place to put them in the hospital," Stan told him. "Where they wouldn't see them, and where you could play with them."

"Thank you," Toby grinned.

Stan stood. "Thank me when I am able to put them here for you."

"I'll say thank you now," Toby responded. "Because no one thought to bring me any toys."

"Others have seen you?"

"Sure," Toby nodded. "There have been plenty. Most of the time, they hide from me. Anyway, I'm sorry about Adam. It'll be easy when he goes, though. I mean, he should be ready for it."

"We will make it as easy as possible," Stan told the dead boy. "I will keep coming in, and I will speak with him about it."

Toby smiled. "That's good. He can hear you, you know."

"I did not know," Stan admitted. "But I hoped. I hoped he could."

Toby looked up at him. "Do you want me to walk you to the door?"

"Yes," Stan said after a moment. "I would like that very much."

In silence, he and the dead boy walked down the stairs and through the hospital.

CHAPTER 34

ANSWERING THE PHONE

Winston didn't remember to turn his phone on until he sat down in his chair with a fresh bottle of beer. He dug the cell phone out of his pocket and turned it on. When it came online, it chimed to show he had a message from Mr. Pettigrew.

Winston thumbed it open and saw, *Call me.*

He took a long pull off the bottle and then called Mr. Pettigrew.

"Winston," Mr. Pettigrew said by way of greeting. "We have a problem regarding the most recent fatality."

"Is that so?" Winston asked, keeping his voice calm as a tremor ripped through him. He recognized it as the final purge of adrenaline from his system, but he still didn't appreciate it.

"Yes. It appears the man killed was another friend of Stan Owens. Important enough, I'm afraid, that Owens reached out via the ads and informed me as much."

"Ah." Winston took another drink.

"I want you to speak with the three ghosts you have," Mr. Pettigrew continued. "Be sure they understand I do not want anyone killed. Accidents happen, so I won't be terribly upset should someone die in the process of being frightened. But we cannot have what happened with the last death."

"That won't be a problem, sir," Winston replied.

"Do you have a good relationship with them?" Mr. Pettigrew asked. "If so, that's wonderful. If not, please, Winston, attempt to cultivate one."

Winston let out a short laugh. "It's not about whether we work well together or not, Mr. Pettigrew. The three ghosts are gone."

There was a moment of silence before Mr. Pettigrew asked, "Have they run off or refused to work anymore?"

"That would be easier to deal with," Winston stated. He finished his drink and held the empty bottle on his lap. "No. They've been obliterated."

"By whom?!" Mr. Pettigrew demanded.

"A Mister Jonathan Coffin," Winston answered. "He killed, if that's the right word, all three of them. The last one he did right in front of me. I don't know why, Mr. Pettigrew, but this one shook me."

"Did you kill him?" Mr. Pettigrew snapped.

Winston snorted out a laugh. "He's already dead."

"What?"

"Coffin is a ghost," Winston said, getting to his feet and carrying the empty bottle out into the kitchen. He set it on the counter by the sink before taking another beer from the refrigerator. "He's dead, Mr. Pettigrew. He's a ghost, and he backtracked Raul, the last ghost of the trio you sent, and he beat him to death, or whatever it is that happens to the dead, so they don't exist anymore. And when he finished, Mr. Pettigrew, when Coffin finished, he told me he didn't want me around anymore."

"This is absurd," Mr. Pettigrew muttered after a moment. "Why would he do that? Why would one ghost attack another?"

"He said that Owens had warned him and others, I guess, about what we were up to."

Mr. Pettigrew didn't respond.

Winston opened the second beer, drank a little and suggested, "Maybe it's time to be a little more direct with Mr. Owens, sir."

Mr. Pettigrew cleared his throat. "What are you suggesting?"

"I'm suggesting, sir, that maybe I just go and talk to him in my own special way."

Another pause filled the air between them.

"Do it somewhere quiet," Mr. Pettigrew stated. "I don't want anyone overhearing your conversation."

"Don't worry," Winston replied. "They never do."

CHAPTER 35

CONVERSATION STARTERS

Mr. Coffin had given Stan an excellent description of the man who had been with the ghost who had partaken in the killing of Noah Yollen. He had even given Stan the numbers on the license plate.

Stan didn't bother bringing the plate number to Sheriff Bowman. Even if the plate was legitimate, he suspected the name it was registered under would be false.

What was most important was the description of the man, and Stan had asked Mr. Coffin and Penny Jones to help spread the word amongst the dead. Should they see him, someone was to get word to Stan.

Stan would take care of it from there.

Stan took off his suitcoat, hung it on a peg in his small workroom and then went to the far side of the barn. An old ladder nailed to the wall and, looking far weaker than it was, stretched into the darkness above. He didn't need lights, though. He knew exactly where he was going.

He climbed the ladder for ten feet straight up, and then he lifted his left hand and pushed a hidden door in the ceiling up and to the side. Motion sensor lights in the small attic flickered into life as he entered and illuminated the shelves as well as the plastic boxes they housed.

Stan crossed the room and pulled a large box off the shelf, setting it down on the floor in front of him. He released the catches, opened the lid and removed a pair of brass knuckles. They were old and scuffed. These were his from his youth, and as he had grown older, he had bored out the fingerholes, making sure the brass still fit and that they didn't lose their integrity.

The metal, cold and heavy in his hands, reminded him of beatings he had delivered at the orders of his granduncle. There was a distinct sound that occurred when brass struck human flesh and bone. It was faintly reminiscent of someone beating a side of beef with a wooden bat.

If he closed his eyes, Stan knew he would be able to feel the splatter of blood on his face and feel the shock of each blow he delivered.

But Stan didn't close his eyes.

There was no need to.

All he needed to do was wait until one of the ghosts saw the stranger who had helped kill Noah Yollen. And then, he intended to have a lengthy conversation.

Winston pulled into a back street, parked the truck and got out, whistling as he did so. There was no need to be sneaky or look like he was doing anything other than what he was doing, which was parking a truck and walking toward Mason's poor excuse for a downtown.

He had made certain to be as far from the place where Raul had been destroyed by Mr. Coffin. The last thing he wanted was for Mr. Coffin to come after him with that war club.

Winston didn't think he would come out on top of that deal. Plus, he didn't know if the ghost was on the lookout for him. And that was something else he really didn't want. Winston had been around the townfolk long enough to hear stories about Stan Owens, and none of them were comforting. Stan had some sort of connection to the dead; everyone talked about it. He seemed to have a way to get them to leave people alone.

And Winston was certain that worked both ways. If Stan could get them to leave people alone, then Stan could get them to hurt someone.

No, Winston didn't want any of that. None of it.

All he wanted was to catch Stan Owens alone and kill him. It was what should have been done in the first place, something he should have advocated for. He had been seduced by the idea of easy money, and like anything else that was easy, you ended up paying for it in the end.

Winston slipped his hands into his pockets and considered the best way to kill Owens. From what he had gathered, the man had served some time in the Army but had been injured and sent home. Medically discharged. Winston had also learned that Owens occasionally got into some scuffles, but nothing too serious. Hick folk crap with a night in the drunk tank.

A knife would do the trick, Winston decided as he paused at a corner. A knife between the ribs, and then he could pack up the body and dump it somewhere in the backwoods.

Winston stepped out into the street and saw Stan Owens turn right ahead of him, and a smile spread across his face.

Times like this, Winston believed someone was looking out for him.

✳ ✳ ✳

"He is following you," Penny advised.

"Thank you," Stan murmured.

"Do you want any more help?" Penny asked. "I mean, I could probably do something to him."

"No, thank you. I will speak with you later."

"Good luck," she whispered and winked.

As Penny left, Stan turned left onto Maple Street and walked to number eighteen, and went into the backyard. He used his key on the backdoor, went inside, turned on the lights and the small television, and then stepped back into the kitchen. Standing by the door, he slipped his hands into the brass knuckles and waited.

✳ ✳ ✳

Winston stood in the backyard of the house at 18 Maple Street. The light from the kitchen window shone down into the yard but didn't touch where he was. He had been there for nearly ten minutes, considering when it would be best to go in.

The house was an enigma.

Did Stan Owens own it? Did he have a lady friend? Was he talking to a ghost inside?

Winston couldn't answer the question about ownership. He doubted anyone would be able to. From what he had gathered, Stan didn't own anything other than a house he never went to, and no one talked about why.

As for a lady friend, there wasn't a car in the driveway. Not only no car, but a quick check of the trash barrel showed it was empty. Same thing with the recycling bin. If anyone occupied the house, they hadn't for at least a week or two.

Winston suspected it was the third option, a ghost. One that hadn't arrived yet, considering the lights and the sound of the television from the front of the small house.

Knowing what he did of Owens, Winston could picture the man sitting in a chair, watching television and waiting for the ghost to make an appearance.

Getting rid of the dead, it seemed, was how Owens made a living.

Making people dead was how Winston earned his.

Winston waited another ten minutes, then eased up the steps to the back door, tested the knob and found it was unlocked. He slipped his knife out of its sheath and entered the house.

Stan watched the doorknob turn, impressed with the patience of the killer on the other side. Almost twenty-five minutes had passed, and here the man was, moving forward with the assault.

Stan didn't imagine anything about the man. He didn't have to.

All he wanted was to question him, and therefore, all he had to do was stop the man and take him prisoner. More than likely, the stranger was going to try and kill him. It was the only step that made sense. The attacks on the townspeople had failed to frighten Stan. The deaths had failed to cow him. Mr. Pettigrew would not believe a beating would work.

Which left only assassination.

The door opened inch by inch, and finally, the assassin stepped in on silent feet.

The man wore jeans and work boots, a flannel shirt and a trucker's cap. His face was nondescript and could be any face in a crowd. In his left hand, he held a long, thin knife, and he held it like he knew how to use it.

Stan had no doubt that the man did.

But it wouldn't matter.

Stan's first punch sought the assassin's right shoulder, the brass slamming into the muscle and deadening it.

The assassin spun on his heel, the blade flashing in the kitchen light, and Stan's second punch smashed into the man's left wrist, shattering it and sending the knife spinning out across the floor. Pain flared up on the man's face, but he still attempted to drive a knee up into Stan's groin.

But Stan had grown up fighting, and he knew the tricks of the trade. Especially the ones designed to make you open to a death strike.

Stan shifted his thigh to take the blow from the assassin's knee and punched the man first in the right side, then the left, ribs cracking with each blow.

Understanding broke over the man's face. The assassin knew now that Stan could fight.

More importantly, he knew Stan was going to win.

The assassin tried to throw himself through the door, but Stan kicked it shut, and the man ended up ramming his head into the door frame instead. The assassin staggered back, uttered a weak snarl and threw himself at Stan, trying to headbutt him and swinging his shattered wrist at him.

Stan blocked the blow and punched the assassin in the groin with enough force to lift him up onto his toes. The man's eyes widened, and he vomited, staggered, and then slipped in his own bile. Stan watched the man try to catch himself with his broken hand, which only resulted in a limp grab for the edge of the counter.

The result was not what Stan or the assassin wanted.

The man's head bounced off the corner of the sink, a resounding crack filling the room.

Stan watched as the assassin sagged and collapsed.

He listened as the man's breathing became shallow, rattling in his chest.

Stan sat down in a chair at the small kitchen table, took off his brass knuckles and held them in his hands.

"It is a shame," Stan told the dying man. "I had hoped for a better fight. I enjoy it, you know. You came in well, but not good enough. You did not expect anything from me, and so you did not come in with the right mindset. You were prepared to kill me. It is unfortunate you were not prepared for me to be ready to kill you. It would have been more entertaining if you were. If you can hear me, understand this, you are dying. This pleases me, sir, as few other things do."

Long, ragged breaths filled the room, and slowly, the breathing stopped.

Stan stood up and went down into the basement. He searched for a short time, and after a while, he found an old blue tarp. It had never been used, and the wrapping crinkled and cracked as Stan opened it.

An additional search resulted in bungee cords, and he suspected that if he dug around a little more, he would find a hacksaw and a package of blades.

His granduncle had been prepared for every eventuality. Even at his mistress's home.

Stan carried the items up to the kitchen, put them on the table and retreated to the bathroom. In the small closet, on the floor beneath shelves of linens, he located the cleaning products.

✳ ✳ ✳

It was close to midnight when Stan finished cleaning the kitchen and had the assassin's body wrapped in the tarp and secured with bungee cords.

Fortunately, the man had not been very large, and so he was not difficult to carry.

Standing in the backyard of the house, with the body at his feet, Stan looked at Penny Jones.

"He deserved it," she stated, looking at the tarp-wrapped corpse.

"Most do."

"I heard from Mr. Coffin," she smiled. "He said the Coffins will let you know if anyone starts walking toward you. Same thing with the Lavoies. They even have that little Le Brei kid running up and down along the path you said you were going to take. It's for the cameras, right?"

"Yes, thank you, Penny," Stan said, offering her a short bow. "You have been most helpful, as always. I did speak with Mr. Coffin for you."

"You did?" she asked, clapping her hands excitedly. "What did he say?"

"He told me he did not know whether a ghost could go 'a courting' as he said, but was certainly most interested in doing so. He referred to you as comely and of having quite the entertaining wit."

Penny frowned. "Is any of that good?"

Stan smiled. "It means he finds you attractive and funny, Penny."

"Oh, Stanley Owens, if I could still blush, I would!" She waved goodbye and hurried away.

Stan squatted down, lifted the corpse up and onto his shoulder. It was less than two miles to Philomena's, but it was through woods and in the darkness. And even when he was at Philomena's, he wouldn't be able to rest. He would need to get the body to the warehouse, and once there, it would be time to send Mr. Pettigrew another message.

One a little firmer than the message he had sent the other day.

With a sigh, he began his trek. He didn't want rigor mortis to set in while he was walking. That would make the situation unnecessarily difficult.

✳ ✳ ✳

Ezra drummed his fingers on the desk and stared at his phone.

Winston should have called. He should have reported that the job was done and that Stan Owens was no longer an issue.

But there hadn't been any call, and Ezra didn't want to disrupt the man by sending a text.

Ezra stopped his fingers and picked up his phone on the off chance that he hadn't heard the alert.

There was nothing. Nothing but the time.

Twelve past midnight. Twelve-twelve.

Winston should have given him a call at least by ten, ten thirty at the latest.

But he hadn't.

Something had gone wrong, and Ezra couldn't deny it.

Questions popped up at random. Did a ghost attack Winston? Did Winston fail in the attempt to kill Owens? Did Winston get injured?

Ezra had no way of knowing, and it was driving him crazy.

With a grunt of frustration, he pushed himself to his feet and walked to the couch on the right side of his office. He would sleep there until the call came in, and if it didn't come in by morning, he would find a way to get the information he needed.

CHAPTER 36
A ROUGH SORT OF MESSAGE

Stan sat in the basement of Philomena's house, and the ghost of his grandaunt had finally given him some peace.

The assassin's corpse was tied to a chair a few feet away, and on an old folding table, the dead man's belongings were laid out. They consisted of a wallet, the knife with which he had tried to kill Stan, a watch, and a cell phone. The phone was turned off, and with Philomena somewhere else on the property, Stan would be able to turn it on.

But not yet.

He picked up the wallet and extracted each item carefully.

There was a New Hampshire driver's license for John Smith with the assassin's photo and signature. Two hundred dollars made up of eight twenties and four tens. A house key was tucked behind a bank card, also in the name of John Smith. The last item was a credit card, too, for John Smith.

Stan picked up the knife, slid it out of its sheath and examined it with a critical eye.

The blade was finely honed and well-cared for, modeled after the weapon the British SAS carried into battle. For a moment, Stan wondered what the provenance of the knife was.

With a shrug, he resheathed the blade and set it down on the table.

Standing up, he walked to the corpse and made certain it looked proper. He had taken the time to seat the body, hands bound behind the back of the chair, ankles clearly tied to the chair legs. The corpse's head hung down, and the eyes were closed. If someone were in the room, they would be able to tell it was a body and not a living man in the chair.

A photograph, though, might lie.

Stan returned to his seat, sat down and picked up the dead man's cell phone. He powered it up, saw it needed a fingerprint scan and got to his feet once more. He walked around to the back, took hold of the dead man's stiff finger and used it to unlock the phone.

Message alerts flashed onto the screen, and Stan ignored them. Instead, he stepped back and took several pictures of the dead man. When he was sitting down again, he looked at the different photos, selected the one in which the assassin appeared unconscious instead of dead, and saved that.

With a nod of satisfaction, Stan went to the messages and saw they were all from Mr. Pettigrew.

Message one: *Were you successful?*

Message two: *Winston, I am still waiting to hear from you.*

Message three: *Winston, it is imperative that you contact me as soon as possible. I need to know whether the mission was a success or a failure. Is Stan Owens still a threat?*

There were more messages, and all were in the same vein.

Stan typed in a reply and attached the photo he had chosen. He read it through, to make sure he wasn't misspelling anything, then sent the message.

Three days had passed since Ezra had last heard from Winston.

Three days of a growing, disturbing silence. He had been forced to leave the day-to-day planning to Robert, who was more than capable, but it was a hands-off process that Ezra disliked.

After the first night, Ezra had forced himself to go home and rest, to try and trust the process. Robert and Abigail had said the same thing to him.

He needed to trust in Winston. Winston was the consummate professional, a man who prided himself on getting the job done and getting it done right.

Still, Ezra had sent numerous messages.

None had been answered.

He sat down at his desk, took a sip of coffee, and double-checked the cell phone. It was on, and the volume was up. He turned the phone face down onto the desktop, then focused on his computer. There were plenty of emails in need of a response, decisions to be made and meetings to attend. New Hampshire was a small problem, occupying far too much of his time.

The phone chimed and Ezra jumped in his seat.

Before he could stop himself, he snatched the cell phone up from the desk, turned it over and saw a message from Winston.

Ezra thumbed it, and an image burst into view.

Winston was sitting in a chair, head down, hands behind his back and ankles tied to the chair legs.

A text portion came through a heartbeat later.

I am still a threat, Mr. Pettigrew. Winston is going to help me find you.

Ezra reached out and pressed the button marked 'one' on his office phone.

Robert entered a moment later, a look of concern on his face.

"Are you all right, sir?" Robert asked.

Ezra shook his head and handed the cell phone to Robert.

"Do you think we could find Winston before he gives up any information?" Ezra asked.

"Possibly," Robert said after a moment. "We don't know how long he's been a prisoner, and given his background, I think he should be able to keep quiet for a bit. I don't think we should task his recovery to another outside hire."

Ezra looked at Robert with surprise.

The man handed the phone back. "Send me, sir. If there's a way to find him, I will. Mason is a small town, and it's obvious that Stan Owens has taken the man. From what we've seen in the reports, he doesn't own a vehicle, and he uses taxis and the like to travel. That means he has to be in town with Winston. I can find him, or at least pinpoint where he's likely to be. If you don't want me to attempt a confrontation, that's fine. I'm not as young as I used to be."

Ezra drummed his fingers on the desktop as he considered Robert's suggestion.

"Fine," Ezra nodded. "On one primary condition. You do not, under any circumstances, engage with Stan Owens. Locate and report. That's all. You are far too important to lose, Robert."

"Understood, sir. Should I leave now?"

"Yes," Ezra answered, rubbing at his eyes. "Inform Abigail of the situation. Have her make arrangements for you as you go. Don't let anything slow you down."

"I won't, sir."

Ezra watched Robert leave and hoped all would be well.

When the door closed, Ezra picked up the cell phone, removed the SIM card and snapped it in half. From his desk, he took a container of small tools and began the slow process of disassembling the cell phone.

As he did so, Winston's image remained burned in his mind's eye.

CHAPTER 37

EMPLOYEE OF THE MONTH

Morrigan had neither the time nor the patience to look for haunted items. She also lacked another important skill; the ability to know a haunted item when she saw one.

Lisbeth Olmec, however, enjoyed not only the skill to see the dead but also the patience and time to look for them. The time came mostly from Morrigan and the healthy salary and bonus system she had put in place for Lisbeth.

The two women sat together in the greenhouse connected to the back of Morrigan's facility. They had finished their coffee and a small plate of cookies, and they now enjoyed the pleasant sight of the various plants growing around them.

"I didn't even know you had this place," Lisbeth said. "You spend a lot of time out here?"

Morrigan nodded. "It's relaxing, and it's warm. I don't have a phone or device in here. The entryway is protected by iron in the threshold, so I don't have to worry about any ghosts that might get out."

"Do you think they might harm you?" Lisbeth asked, an expression of professional curiosity on her face.

"No," Morrigan smiled. "I'm more concerned about the plants. I know what a shift in temperature would do to most of them. It wouldn't be pleasant, and neither would I. I've spent a good deal of time bringing each plant back to health."

Lisbeth frowned. "Back to health? Did something happen?"

"Yes, but I'm not sure what," Morrigan answered, picking up a crumb off her slacks and setting it on the plate. "Over the past few months, I've purchased all of these plants from clearance shelves of some of the big box stores. They weren't in the best of shape."

"It sounds like this new hobby is a peaceful one."

Morrigan nodded. "It is. Tell me, how did the trip to New Haven go?"

Lisbeth chuckled. "Oh, that was rough. Some of the shops were a little overpriced. They really thought they were all that."

"Any luck at all?" Morrigan asked, knowing already that Lisbeth had succeeded in obtaining at least one item of note. If she hadn't, then she simply would have texted or emailed that she was still on the hunt. But it was a part of the game they played, the polite question and the equally polite answer.

"A bit," Lisbeth answered, and a devilish grin spreading across her petite features. She brushed a stray forelock of her electric blue hair out of her eyes, chuckled and said, "Five pieces from a shop on Third Street and three from a shop on Fifth Street."

"Five and three, and three and five," Morrigan murmured with satisfaction. A portent that could only have been better if there had been a third collection point.

"I think I would have gotten more," Lisbeth continued. "But the last shop I went to, the owner was on vacation."

"The audacity!" Morrigan declared, laughing.

Lisbeth laughed as well, nodding her head. "From what I saw, the owner hasn't been on vacation in years. At least according to the coffee shop beside it. Evidently, the antique shop owner is a single mom, all that stuff."

"More power to her, then," Morrigan replied.

Lisbeth nodded her agreement.

"So," Lisbeth said a moment later. "Where to next?"

"That's a good question," Morrigan answered. "I even have a good answer for it. It's not so much a where to as it is a what."

Lisbeth raised an eyebrow, the small metal piercing there glinting in the warm rays of light piercing the glass of the greenhouse.

"I need more fighters," Morrigan stated.

"You already sold the Cuban soldiers?" Lisbeth asked, surprised.

"I did," Morrigan smiled. "I think the buyer is going to need more soon, too. He seems a little overly ambitious."

"Okay. That shouldn't be a problem," Lisbeth told her. "I'll head on down to one of the forts."

Morrigan frowned.

Lisbeth laughed. "Soldiers sell their stuff all the time. More importantly, they sell stuff that isn't theirs. It's stuff that belonged to other soldiers, both living and dead, and so sometimes the items in the pawn shops, they're haunted."

"Haunted by soldiers," Morrigan smiled. "That is a brilliant plan."

Lisbeth nodded. "Thank you. Now, can we move a little bit away from the business side of things?"

"Of course," Morrigan answered.

"What's new with you?" Lisbeth asked. "It's been a hot minute since we talked about anything other than work."

"Things are going well. I bumped into an old classmate."

"Who?" Lisbeth asked, putting her elbows on the table and resting her chin in her hands.

"No one you would know, Lisbeth," Morrigan said with a teasing rebuke.

"Rude," Lisbeth sighed theatrically as she straightened up. "Absolutely rude. What do you think mother would say about keeping secrets from your sister?"

"She would say I needed to talk less and that it would go doubly for you," Morrigan answered.

Lisbeth snickered. "Yeah. She would. Anyway, that's cool. Since we're done with the coffee and cookies, do you want to take a look at what I brought back?"

"Absolutely," Morrigan answered.

Together, the two sisters stood, cleared the table and left the warmth of the greenhouse for the chill temperatures of the storage room.

CHAPTER 38

GREELEY PARK

"You look tired, Stan."

Stan blinked and nodded. "I am sorry, Gwen. I have not slept well recently."

"Anything I can help you with?" she asked.

"Your company is help enough," he told her, and Gwen moved a little closer to him on the bench.

They sat in Greeley Park with the late afternoon sun shining down on them. A few children called out to one another as they rode their bikes up a nearby path, and in the distance, Stan heard the rumble of heavy machinery. A diesel truck rumbled by, its exhaust pipes spewing black clouds as the driver revved the engine once they were past the crosswalk.

"This is a nice place," Stan observed. "Thank you for inviting me."

"I like your company, too, Stan," Gwen told him, and she slipped her hand into his.

The touch of her skin against his sent warmth running through him, and his shoulders dropped slightly. He felt a sense of comfort wash over him as his heart picked up its rhythm.

"Do you have a lot of nightmares?" she asked.

Stan considered the question. "Not a lot. I do have them, though. Most of the time, I am fortunate in that I do not remember them."

"Are they about your childhood?" She leaned her head against his shoulder. The smell of her shampoo, sweet and delicate, wrapped around him.

"No," he admitted. "They are primarily about my time in the

Army."

"Is that something you want to talk about?" Gwen glanced up at him. "I don't want to pry."

"It is not prying," Stan told her. "The Army was pleasant for me in the beginning. I enjoyed basic training and advanced training. My unit was laid back and required little to keep itself in order. When the First Gulf War began, we were sent to Iraq, and that is where the pleasantness of my military experience ended."

"You were wounded?"

He nodded. "They refer to it now as an improvised explosive device. I do not think it was anything so intentional. I believe it was nothing more than a trap left behind for someone like me, a soldier tasked with searching the wreckage on the Highway of Death."

"I've seen footage of that," Gwen said. "It looked horrible."

"It was horrible," he confirmed. "And then I was wounded. I survived despite my close proximity to the explosive and despite the amount of shrapnel I took."

"Are your scars from the explosion?" she asked, tracing the thin scars on the back of his hand.

"Yes. I am covered in such scars."

Gwen straightened up, frowning. "What?"

"I was wounded enough to require a flight to Germany and then to Walter Reed Hospital here in the United States," Stan informed her. "They were able to remove a great deal of the shrapnel, but not all of it. I have a special card I carry with me should I need to pass through a metal detector."

"That must have been terrible," she murmured and rested her head on his shoulder once again.

"Many things changed at that point," Stan continued.

"I can only imagine. I don't mean to pry, really, Stan."

"You are not prying, Gwen," he told her. "I do not believe you can."

She squeezed his hand.

They were silent for a short time, and then Stan spoke. "May I tell you something?"

"Of course."

"Something strange happened to me when I was wounded," he began. "One of the doctors believed it was due to the traumatic brain injury caused by the explosion. I can see the dead."

Gwen straightened up and shifted her position on the bench so she could look at him. She still held onto his hand.

"You can see ghosts?" she asked.

He nodded. "I felt you should know this. We seem to be getting closer."

Gwen gave him a crooked smile and lifted his hand to her lips, kissing the back of it gently.

"Yes, we're getting closer. Are you worried I'll think you have mental health issues because you can see ghosts?"

"Yes."

"I believe in ghosts," Gwen told him. "Fully and absolutely. I also believe some people can see them some of the time and that some, a very small minority, can see them all the time."

"I am in that very small minority," he admitted.

"When was the first time you saw a ghost?" she asked.

"At Walter Reed," Stan answered. "I thought I was losing my mind. They brought in an older man who explained what was happening. It was difficult."

"I can only imagine." She paused and then asked, "Is this why everyone listens to you in Mason?"

Stan nodded. "When I returned from the war, I assisted some people with issues they were having regarding the dead. When something arises, centered upon the dead, I am there to help."

"Is that why you don't live at your granduncle's house?" she asked. "Is there a ghost there you don't want to see?"

"Yes," Stan said. "My grandaunt haunts the house, and I do my best to keep her in there. She was a violent woman during her life. She killed at least one person as a ghost, and I would not like to see her death rate increase."

"And so you live at Marilyn's," Gwen murmured. "Do you like it there?"

"I do."

"How much does she charge you, if you don't mind my asking?"

"I do not mind, and she does not charge me anything. I helped her son, and so I live for free. I do chores around the house, though. I dislike feeling as though I am taking advantage of her," Stan stated.

"What did you do that helped her son?" Gwen asked.

Stan shook his head. "I am sorry, Gwen. Marilyn does not wish me to speak of the finer details. He is no longer alive, though, and his passing was made easy. I can tell you that much."

"Don't apologize, Stan," Gwen replied. "I'm glad you can keep secrets, believe it or not. People don't need to know everything, and I can say that as a professional."

"True."

"So," Gwen said, changing the conversation, "what do you do other than help people?"

Stan frowned. "On occasion, I read. However, I have not been able to do so much of late. There have been issues in town, and my focus has been on that."

"What do you like to read?"

"I find comfort in the classics," he admitted. "The books I disliked in school when we were made to read them. And you, Gwen, what do you like to do in your free time?"

"I collect curiosities," she laughed. "I've also discovered a penchant for plants. My office windows are filled with them now. Some of my clients dislike them, but the plants aren't for the clients. They're for me."

"I would like to see them," Stan said. "Especially if they make you happy."

"I have more at home," she sighed, wrapping her free arm around his waist. She held onto him tightly. "I would like to show you those, too."

Stan bent his head and kissed the top of hers.

CHAPTER 39

THE NURSE

She wore an older nurse's uniform, and she was dead.

She did not enjoy the fact that Stan could see her.

They were alone on Pine Street, and it was close to midnight. Trash barrels and recycling bins were lined up at the curb in preparation for the following day's curbside collection.

She took a step closer, a sneer forming on her face.

"You can see me," she declared.

"I can," Stan confirmed. "Is this an issue for you?"

"I don't want you to look at me." She went to the nearest recycling bin and squatted down.

Stan watched, curious as to what she was going to do next.

Her face tightened, anger flared across her features, and she thrust a hand into the bin. A rattle of glass followed, and he watched, surprised, as she lifted an empty wine bottle and stood up.

"Get off this street," she ordered, holding the bottle above her head.

"How did you get into Mason?" he asked, keeping his distance from her.

"None of your damned business!"

The dead woman threw the bottle with more speed and force than Stan had anticipated or even believed possible.

The thick bottom of the bottle struck him in the right thigh, deadening it and causing him to drop to his knee. The impact of the joint on the pavement sent a shock up into his hip, and he gritted his teeth as he forced himself up.

A second bottle hurtled through the night, glinting and flashing in the glow of the street lamps. The bottle struck his forehead and sent him tumbling back. He felt blood spill down the side of his head, and he rolled, forcing himself to get to his feet as a third bottle smashed into the sidewalk, narrowly missing where he had just been.

Stan wavered on his feet, knowing two things instantly.

One, he had a head injury that was more than a cut.

Two, the dead woman could seriously injure him without engaging in close-quarters combat.

He held up his hands and took a step back. "I am leaving your street."

He knew it wasn't hers, and he would deal with her sooner rather than later. Stan did not want anyone to die because he had been injured too much to stop the ghost, and he felt certain she had not only the ability, but also the desire, to kill.

She watched him as he continued to back up. In each hand, she held a wine bottle, and Stan wondered, idly, who drank so much wine that their recycling bin was filled with bottles.

"I'll kill you if you come back," she hissed.

"I believe you," Stan told her.

No more words were exchanged as he backed down the street, occasionally glancing over his shoulder to make sure he didn't trip on anything. At number 8 Pine Street, she stopped following, and Stan made a mental note of that. Either her domain ended there, or she no longer saw him as a threat.

Stan doubted it was the latter.

"How did this happen?" Marilyn asked, washing Stan's wound with alcohol.

Stan kept his eyes closed and ignored the pain as she cleaned and inspected the cut.

"Apparently," Stan answered, "I upset a dead woman on Pine Street."

"I didn't think there were any ghosts there."

"Neither did I," Stan said. "I will have to ask around and see what might have happened. She did not look familiar, and given the state of strange ghosts coming into town, I believe she may have been transported here."

Stan stopped and sighed.

"What is it?" Marilyn asked, applying a bandage to his head and securing it with medical tape.

"I just remembered. One of the attackers was described as a nurse."

"Do you know who the victim was?"

"Yes," Stan answered. He opened his eyes. "Mallory Scanlan."

"Oh, yes, poor Mallory," Marilyn nodded, sitting down in the kitchen chair opposite Stan. Her first aid kit lay open on the table. "I was just at her house today. She's having a devil of a time keeping up with the plants since the attack."

"It would make sense," Stan stated. "Mallory's house would be close to the center of the dead woman's radius."

"What?" Marilyn asked, confused.

"Nothing. I am sorry, Marilyn," Stan apologized. "I was thinking out loud. Thank you very much for your help."

"You know I am always happy to, Stan," Marilyn smiled. Then, her smile faded, and she asked, "Have you been over to see Adam recently?"

"I have," Stan answered, and for a moment, he considered telling her about the younger man's worsening condition. However, he decided not to. "His situation has not changed, unfortunately."

"I had heard as much," she told him. "One can always hope that he wakes up. I think of him often."

"As do I," Stan said. He started to stand and wobbled on his feet.

Marilyn caught hold of his arm and steadied him. "Perhaps you should rest in the parlor for now, Stan. I don't want you climbing the stairs in your condition."

Part of him wanted to argue with her, but he knew she was right.

"If you think it's best," Stan replied and allowed Marilyn to lead him into the parlor. Once she had him seated on the couch, she left and returned a few minutes later with his pillow and a blanket. He undid his shoes, took off his suitcoat and cufflinks, and then stretched out on the couch. Marilyn helped him adjust his pillow, covered him with his blanket and smiled at him.

"Get some rest, Stan," she told him. "I will see you in the morning for tea."

"Thank you, Marilyn."

Stan closed his eyes, and his thoughts drifted to Gwen. He remembered the smell of her hair and the feel of her lips on his hand.

For the first time in years, nightmares did not plague him.

CHAPTER 40
NEW HAMPSHIRE

Robert took an instant dislike to the state of New Hampshire.

The airport in Manchester was small, the people rude, and every native he spoke with sounded as though they were pinching their nose when they talked. And they talked fast. Much faster than he was used to. It wasn't that he couldn't understand what they were saying, it was that they weren't saying anything important enough to be said fast.

He could understand racing through a sentence if someone was in danger, but if he was getting directions to the taxi pick-up outside, there was no reason for ripping through the sentence.

Robert got out of his taxi in front of Somerset Plaza in Nashua, NH, and waited as the driver got his bags for him. The man didn't seem pleased, and so Robert made him even angrier by stiffing him on a tip.

When the man glared at him, Robert merely looked back. "Do better," he told the driver.

The driver swore at him and tore out of the parking lot.

Sighing, Robert pulled his luggage along behind him, entered the hotel and signed in with a minimal amount of fuss, for which he was thankful. The concierge even offered to get a member of staff to help with the baggage, but Robert politely declined, although he did place a ten-dollar tip on the desk.

When she looked at him in surprise, he smiled.

"Just because I don't want assistance doesn't mean your staff should go without a tip. Thank you for your professionalism," he told her, and he walked away.

Robert took the elevator up to the fourth floor, went to his room and sat down on the edge of the bed. There was no reason to text Abigail. She would receive an automatic notification from the hotel saying he had checked in. He also saw no reason to text Mr. Pettigrew, at least not yet.

Robert wanted to get into Mason and get a feel for the town before he sent any information back. He would have to try and locate Stan Owens, and in doing so, he would hopefully get a location for Winston. Robert had no particular love for the hitman, but he did want to protect Mr. Pettigrew, which meant being certain Winston wasn't going to talk and put Mr. Pettigrew in danger.

And Stan Owens was, without any doubt, a dangerous man.

Mr. Pettigrew needed protection, and that was exactly what Robert was going to provide for him. If that meant saving a killer from an interfering New England country bumpkin, then that was what Robert was going to do.

Robert's phone buzzed, and he opened the message.

Second floor of the parking garage. Black Hyundai Sonata, keys are under the driver's seat. Good luck, Abigail.

Robert smiled and texted back, *Thank you.*

Neither he nor Abigail were married. Their dedication was to Mr. Pettigrew and his business, to seeing the man succeed. Robert didn't know why he felt such loyalty to Mr. Pettigrew, and to Abigail for that matter, but both provided him with a sense of purpose and understanding. Robert and Abigail had lost their spouses early in life, and widower and widow had flourished in Mr. Pettigrew's employ.

They both believed it would continue.

They understood that, at times, steps outside of the law needed to be taken. The fact that Mr. Pettigrew sought to utilize ghosts now showed what a forward thinker he was. It was forward thinking that would lead the country into the next century, and Robert and Abigail wanted that to happen.

Robert stood up, stretched and then walked back to his luggage.

He transferred the contents from each bag to the dresser and the closet, and when he was finally settled in, he took a long shower to wash off the ache of travel.

He didn't mind flying so much as he minded the people he flew with. His tolerance for the stupidity and arrogance of other travelers was at a bare minimum. Flying reminded him of his wife's death when her car had slid on black ice and crashed through a guardrail before tumbling down an embankment and into a frozen pond.

He let the memory of his wife come and go, then dried off and dressed himself. His stomach rumbled, and he decided it was time to eat. There was an Applebee's in a nearby shopping plaza, and it was as good a place as any to get something solid to eat.

Robert made sure he had everything he needed, then left to get the keys out of the car. He would walk to the restaurant just to let his legs stretch, but he wanted to have the keys. The last thing he wanted was to have the car stolen.

Mr. Pettigrew didn't need any additional expenses.

It was his third cup of coffee, and it was just as disgusting as the previous two. For a moment, Robert wondered why it was so difficult for a diner to make a decent cup of coffee. Was it a requirement that they make only bad coffee? Was there a specific brand of coffee that they were forced to purchase and brew?

Robert sighed, picked up another packet of sugar, shook it, and then tore the end off. He added the sugar to the coffee, stirred it in with a battered flatware spoon, and took a sip. The added sweetness smothered another small portion of the coffee's bitterness, but not nearly enough.

Still, Robert kept a smile on his face as the waitress passed by and the local sheriff entered with a female deputy. The two of them took the booth directly behind Robert, and he listened as the two fell into an easy conversation.

"Did you see him this morning?" the deputy asked.

"No, but I spoke with Marilyn," the sheriff answered. "She said it was a deep gash. She cleaned it as best she could and wrapped it. She thinks it might need stitches."

"He already took care of it," the deputy stated.

"How's that?"

"Apparently, he went and bought the first aid glue and just about coated the wound in it. I told him there'd be another scar there if he didn't get it looked at by a professional," the deputy added.

The sheriff chuckled. "That's definitely not something Stan Owens will ever worry about."

"How did he get all those scars?" the deputy asked, and Robert listened closer.

"An injury when he was in Iraq," the sheriff answered.

"Isn't he too old to have been in Iraq?" the deputy asked.

The sheriff chuckled. "The First Iraq War, or Persian Gulf War. Whatever it's called. That was back in ninety-one. Long before you were born."

"Ha ha, very funny, Sheriff," the deputy said. "I didn't know there was a First Iraq War. You said he was wounded?"

"Yes," the sheriff answered. "And when he was better, he came home. I don't know why, though."

"Yeah."

The conversation stopped as the diner's waitress left the kitchen and came out to take the sheriff and the deputy's orders. The three of them chatted pleasantly for a minute, and then the waitress stopped by Robert.

"Do you need anything?" she asked.

"If you have any chocolate pie left, I would love a slice of that," Robert lied. He would eat it, but he suspected it would be just as terrible as the coffee.

"We do," she smiled.

Behind him, the conversation picked up where it had left off.

"Did they ever find anything solid on his granduncle?" the deputy asked.

"No, that man was too smart for anyone. Nobody really knows how much he had in money or real estate or anything else, for that matter. I've heard rumors as to what Stan went through, too. They make horror movies about that stuff."

"I wouldn't have come back here," the deputy muttered. "It would be like being back in your worst nightmare every day."

"I know," the sheriff agreed. "But he did. He made a point to help, too."

"I was little when he came back," the deputy said after a minute. "My parents, they didn't like hearing all the ghost talk. It scared them."

"Most of the town was scared back then," the sheriff told her. "Not just your parents. The dead seemed to run this place at times, and it surely wasn't a good thing."

"Here's your pie," the waitress said, and Robert nearly jumped off his seat.

"Are you okay?" she asked, her eyes wide.

"Yes," Robert nodded. He smiled sheepishly. "I was daydreaming. Caught me off guard. I'm sorry."

"No need to apologize," she assured him. "I hope the pie is as good as it looks. I haven't had a chance to sample it today, and I probably shouldn't." She winked playfully at him. "I need to drop a few pounds, and I think I gain weight just looking at those pies."

Robert gave her a genuine smile. His wife used to joke the same way. "Understood."

Behind him, the conversation had continued.

"Well, he helped out with Marilyn's son, and that was a hell of a mess," the sheriff was explaining. "And you know all about Maddie

Burnwell's case."

"I still can't wrap my head around that sometimes," the deputy said. "And I was there. I was right there, Paul. I saw the ghost take that girl, I saw them vanish into that closet like there was a great big hall beyond it. And then you brought Stan in. He didn't even stop. Didn't hesitate. He walked right into the closet and closed the door behind him."

"How long did it take him?"

"Five minutes," the deputy answered. "Five minutes to get that girl back. She was unconscious, you know. Her hair was white. Eleven years old and her hair was white. Neither of them talked about what went on in there, and you know what, I'm okay with that."

"You should be. Everyone should be. I've been there before when Stan was getting ready to do something. And I've left when he told me to."

The waitress came out of the kitchen with the lunch order for the sheriff and the deputy. As she served them, Robert picked up his fork and took a bite of the chocolate pie.

It was surprisingly good.

CHAPTER 41

PINE STREET

Despite the pain in his head, Stan stood at 6 Pine Street, knowing that with only a few steps, he would be back in the radius of the dead nurse who had harmed Mallory Scanlan. His own injuries weren't anything that bothered him. He had suffered worse, and the injuries the dead woman had caused were because he hadn't been treating her as a significant threat.

But now he was.

He knew she had the ability to throw physical objects. This led to the distinct possibility that she might have moved her own item to someplace safe. But that was only if she considered him a threat, and Stan hoped she did not.

He had also spent a significant amount of time thinking about the location of her item. If Mallory was the dead nurse's first and only known victim, there was a chance the dead woman's item could be close to Mallory's home. The only way he would learn that, however, would be through another confrontation with the dead woman.

Stan took a deep, cleansing breath and walked past number 6 Pine Street. He passed 8, 10, 12 and made it as far as 62 before the dead woman appeared.

Fortunately for him, the trash and recycling had been collected, and she did not have a ready supply of ammunition at hand. There were plenty of smaller items, rocks and sticks and the like, but he would deal with those as they came.

"I told you to stay off my street," she snarled.

"So you did," Stan agreed, and he did not stop advancing on her.

The dead nurse glanced around, obviously searching for something to throw, and when she did, Stan quickened his pace.

As she squatted down and her hand latched onto a fist-sized rock, Stan reached her.

She looked up, a feral, foul grin on her face.

The dead woman did not suspect him of being able to interfere with her.

And that was fine.

She opened her mouth to speak, and Stan kicked her.

Cold swept over him as she vanished, the rock dropping with a thunk as it struck the earth. Without any hesitation, Stan continued down the street.

He reached the intersection with Walnut, crossed it, and saw the dead woman coming out of a house at the corner of Walnut and Emerson. She saw him, snatched up a stone and hurled it at him.

Her aim from that distance was terrible, and the rock passed over him harmlessly.

"Did you put iron in your boots?" she demanded, searching for another object to throw.

Stan didn't answer.

"Good luck kicking me now," she spat and leaped at him.

Stan gave her a backhand that numbed his hand and caused her to disappear. He turned left at the corner of Walnut and Emerson, and ahead, he saw Mallory's home.

A heartbeat later, the dead woman came out of the side yard of the house next to Mallory's.

The nurse saw him, and her eyes widened.

"What are you?!" she demanded, taking a step back into the yard.

Stan quickened his pace, and she turned and ran.

By the time he reached the sideyard, he saw the dead woman furiously trying to dig. In her panic, she lacked the concentration needed to move something as fine as dirt.

Whoever had placed her object had hidden it just enough to stop her, although Stan doubted that was the intent.

The dead woman twisted around, manic and fear in her eyes.

"Don't take it!" she hissed. "I'm out, and I'm free. Leave me alone!"

Stan reached out and touched her, and the nurse shrieked as she vanished.

Kneeling, Stan moved some of the dirt, and when she reappeared, he swiped at her lazily, knocking her back into nothingness. Before she could come forward again, he picked up a dirty paperweight and slipped it into a protective, iron-laced bag. He cinched it closed and got to his feet.

Stan's head throbbed, and he tightened his grip on the bag. He needed to get to Marilyn's so he could gather up his keys and call for a ride.

It was time to visit the warehouse.

CHAPTER 42

DESTRUCTION

Stan sat in near-complete darkness.

It reminded him of his youth and of the terrible things he had done for his granduncle. He found the thoughts significant as he looked at the dead nurse standing in front of him, trapped in the iron square.

"What are you going to do with me?" she asked, her voice cold.

She had already tried to escape, and she had seen the weight hoisted above her paperweight.

When he didn't answer, she picked up the paperweight and looked at him.

"I could throw this and escape, you know," she remarked.

Stan remained silent.

"What would you do?" she asked. "Just pick it up and put it back in here?"

Stan reached out to the post where the belaying pin waited for his hand, but instead of pulling it, he flipped a switch.

Bright light flooded the warehouse, reflected in thousands of granules of salt and rock salt spread across the floor. It spread nearly thirty yards in every direction.

The dead woman laughed and set her paperweight down.

Stan turned off the overhead lights.

She sat down crisscrossed on the floor and folded her arms over her chest.

"Now what?" she asked.

"Now," Stan said, "I decide if I destroy slowly or quickly."

"Are you a sadist?" she leered.

"At times."

She nodded. "Fair enough. You disapprove of me attacking you?"

He shook his head, and she frowned.

"You're a masochist, too?" she asked.

"No. I am vengeful," he told her. "You harmed someone who did nothing to anyone."

The dead woman laughed. "I used to kill babies that annoyed me."

"Were you killed for that?"

"They never caught me," she replied.

"How did you die?"

"That's not your business," she told him. "Not your business at all. Are you going to destroy me?"

"Soon," Stan confirmed.

"All because I hurt someone in your town? What was she, an old girlfriend or something?"

"No."

The nurse frowned. "Then why do you even care about what I did?"

"Mason is my town," he told her. "I do not enjoy it when people are injured in my town. Especially when those injuries are caused by the dead."

"Do you think I care about what upsets you?" she asked, laughing.

"No. Why would I?"

"Why else would you tell me?" the dead woman said.

"Because you asked the question."

"You tell the truth all the time?"

Stan considered the question, then replied, "No. There are times when a lie must be told. I try to keep those times to a bare minimum."

"So, you're going to finish me off, then?"

"Yes."

She nodded and sat down on the floor. "Do you know if there's an afterlife?"

"I do not."

"Do you want there to be one?" she asked him.

"I do not know," Stan told her. "I do not know if it is comforting to think of one who sits in judgment or not. I have done many terrible things to people. I will do more. Should I be judged for those actions?"

"I don't know," the dead woman stated.

"Neither do I."

"If there's a Hell," she said, "think I'll see you there?"

"Yes," Stan nodded, and he pulled the belaying pin.

Robert had spent three days, start to finish, searching through the town of Mason for any sign of Winston. And while he hadn't learned anything about the man, Robert had been presented with a master's course on Stan Owens.

Stan was a far more violent and dangerous man than he had suspected, and Robert didn't believe Mr. Pettigrew knew any of Stan Owens' personal history.

At the start of the fourth day of searching, just when Robert was about to give up the quest, he came upon the truck Abigail had purchased for Winston at the behest of Mr. Pettigrew. A quick check of the VIN number confirmed the vehicle.

The truck was located in a small bit of woods roughly a mile from the lodging house where Stan Owens lived.

If Winston had managed to escape from Stan Owens, he would have returned to the truck.

The same if Owens had let the man go.

Winston, Robert felt certain, was dead.

He didn't bother searching the town again. Instead, he drove back to the hotel, returned to his room and called Mr. Pettigrew.

"Robert," Mr. Pettigrew greeted when he answered the phone.

"What news from the hinterlands?"

"Nothing good, I'm afraid, sir."

Mr. Pettigrew sighed. "I wasn't expecting good news. Hopeful, but not expectant."

"I don't believe Winston is alive, sir."

"Why is that?" Mr. Pettigrew asked.

"I haven't seen any sign of him in Mason or at the house. There haven't been bodies found, and there aren't any John Doe's in any of the hospitals within a fifty-mile radius. Finally, sir, I located his truck today."

"Is there any chance he's alive?" Mr. Pettigrew asked.

"Of course, there's also a slight chance," Robert told him. "However, I don't believe we're going to find him alive. I will be surprised if we find any trace of him whatsoever."

"Why is that?" Mr. Pettigrew asked. "Stan Owens didn't seem like a terribly dangerous individual."

"I didn't think so at first either, sir," Robert agreed. "I've acquired some additional information about him, though. He is, to put it bluntly, far more dangerous than we could have believed."

"How so?"

Robert told him.

It took almost two hours to tell everything Robert had learned, and when he did, he waited for Mr. Pettigrew's response.

"This is far more than I expected," Mr. Pettigrew admitted. "I need to think about this."

"Is there anything more you want me to do?" Robert asked.

"Stay there and continue to visit Mason," Mr. Pettigrew replied. "I want you to try to learn Stan Owen's movements and habits. Do not confront him, Robert. He is far too dangerous, and I need time to decide what I'm going to do next. Is that understood?"

"Perfectly, sir. Is there anything else you would like me to do while I gather the information?"

"I want you to stay safe, Robert," Mr. Pettigrew answered. "You are far too important to lose. We'll hire a professional to speak with Stan Owens if necessary."

"Pardon me, sir, but Winston was a professional."

"True," Mr. Pettigrew sighed. "But apparently, he wasn't professional enough."

CHAPTER 43
EDUCATIONAL PURPOSES ONLY

Ezra found himself in a peculiar situation. One he didn't enjoy.

Robert was engaged in tracking Stan Owens, a man who was proving to be far more difficult to remove than should have been possible. Not only that, the assassin Ezra had hired was missing, presumably still held prisoner by Owens. Finally, none of the ghosts he had spent a significant amount of money on had lasted as long as he had hoped they would.

And, per his last conversation with Morrigan, violent ghosts were the exception and not the rule.

Ezra wondered, though, if the rules could be changed. He had changed a significant amount of them himself over the years, especially those related to businesses and their operations in small towns. The solution to those problems had been money, and with the dissolution of one of his companies, Ezra found himself with a significant amount of liquid capital.

He would need to purchase more ghosts from Morrigan, but he would need to speak with her about violent ghosts again. He had a question he hoped she could answer. All he had to do was phrase it properly and hope her phone lines were as secure as his own.

Ezra took out a pad of paper and a pen, and began jotting down ideas as to how best to present his question. Asking in the right way almost always resulted in the desired answer.

Almost always.

Leaning over the pad, Ezra bent his will to the task.

✳ ✳ ✳

Morrigan stood by the phone, waited until the third ring ended and picked it up before the fourth could begin.

"Good evening," she said.

"Morrigan, it's Ezra Pettigrew."

"Hello, Ezra," she greeted. "What can I help you with this evening?"

The man chuckled, cleared his throat and asked, "Well, I have a bit of a theoretical question for you."

"Theoretical?" Morrigan asked. "Regarding the dead?"

"Of course."

"Well, let's hear your theoretical then," she told him.

"As you know, I've been in need of violent ghosts," Ezra began. "Specifically, violent ghosts with a penchant for murder, if so directed."

"Yes."

"I seem to have run into a problem, and it is a problem caused by my demand and the thinness of the supply," he concluded.

"Yes. What is your theoretical question, then, Ezra?"

"Is there a way to make a violent ghost?" he asked.

Morrigan blinked. "You want to make a violent ghost?"

"Not necessarily me," Ezra stated hastily. "I am assuming there are natural occupations that would lead one to be violent. Police officers, soldiers, and even gang members are all in naturally violent occupations. Now, police officers rarely die in the line of duty, and for that, we should all be thankful."

Ezra chuckled on the other end of the line and then continued with his line of thought. "Soldiers die quite frequently, unfortunately. Granted, the United States has drawn back as of late, but we should fully expect the country to be immersed in some sort of foreign conflict sooner rather than later. Gang members, especially in the larger cities, die at a disturbingly high rate. So, my question is, could an individual, or perhaps a small team, be sent out to places of violence? Places where death is not only a possibility, but a probability. Couldn't then the body be removed and brought to a facility where a sensitive could keep an eye on it? See if perhaps a ghost appears. If that doesn't work, then would it be possible to discover those who have a greater likelihood of becoming a ghost?"

"Are you asking if there is a way to identify violent people who might become ghosts?" Morrigan asked.

"Yes," Ezra confirmed.

"There is not a way that I know of," Morrigan informed him, not bothering to hide her distaste for the conversation.

"And that brings me to my next question," Ezra continued, oblivious to her tone. "What if violent individuals were brought to a secure and prepared location?"

"What would be done at this secure facility?" Morrigan asked, speaking through clenched teeth.

"Well, the subjects would be tested repeatedly by people trained to observe and correlate data," Ezra told her. "There are plenty of individuals who are sociopathic enough so that this task wouldn't bother them. We would need to be careful and not engage any psychopaths. There shouldn't be any torture for the sake of torture. But, when enough evidence was gathered, the test subject would be put down, humanely, if that would allow for the creation of the ghost, violently if not. Then, with the test subject physically eliminated, observations could be made, and, hopefully, a proper method for the creation of a violent ghost could be documented."

"Mr. Pettigrew," Morrigan started, "I deal with the dead. I do not create them. Ghosts are a natural result of the world. I will not, and I cannot emphasize this enough, create a ghost. Either intentionally or unintentionally. It is not akin to murder, Mr. Pettigrew, it *is* murder.

Regardless of whatever terminology you use, it is murder, and I will have no part of it. Should you need additional ghosts, Mr. Pettigrew, I will do my best to provide them. Other than that, you need to keep your theories to yourself. Now, if you will excuse me, I have work to do."

Morrigan hung up and turned away from the phone, disgusted with what the man had said.

✳ ✳ ✳

Ezra frowned and closed his phone. He took a sip of water, then shook his head with disbelief.

He had felt certain the woman would have agreed. Not only was it a solid concept for the possible control and creation of a violent ghost, it would have been a sure money-maker for the woman.

Apparently, she had no head for business.

Ezra, however, did.

He opened his laptop, created a new folder and then a new document, and titled it Business Plan for Ghost Origination.

He selected a template, settled back in his chair and typed out the initial business proposal. It would need to be edited, of course, but he could go back to that later.

The important part was to get it down on paper first.

Humming, Ezra typed in the stillness of the office.

CHAPTER 44

THE BODY

"Are you going to leave it here to rot?" Philomena asked.

Stan glanced at his dead grandaunt before shaking his head. "No. That is not my intention."

"Then what is your intention?"

"To dispose of it," Stan answered.

"Do you even remember how to do that?" A sneer curled her lips, and Stan focused once more on the assassin's body.

"Yes," Stan said absently. "How do you forget something like that?"

"That was sarcasm, Stanley," his grandaunt snapped. "Your lack of ability to recognize sarcasm was one of your many idiosyncrasies that irritated me when I was alive."

"And now?" Stan asked. "Do they still bother you?"

"Irritate," she corrected. "And yes, on occasion, they do. I try not to think about them, though. I'm more focused on escaping from the house. At least for a little bit."

"Ah."

"How long do you think it will take?" she asked.

"I do not know," Stan answered. "I must decide what message I am sending first."

"Mail his head. That generally works. Or at least it did for your granduncle."

Stan nodded his agreement. "Yes, but that was in a time when he could have it hand delivered to the person he wanted to intimidate. Unfortunately, I do not know where Ezra Pettigrew is, and so I must rely on the postal service. Thus, I believe I must take photos of the body and send them in."

"Didn't you already take pictures?" his grandaunt asked.

"Yes," Stan confirmed. "In them, though, he almost looked alive. With the new pictures, I want there to be no doubt that his assassin is dead. Mr. Pettigrew needs to understand this. I do not believe it will move him to caution or withdrawal from Mason, but I do not want to rule out the slight possibility that it might work."

Philomena looked at the body.

"There's no doubt now," she stated.

The assassin's body lay on its side, legs still bound to the chair and hands still behind its back. Blood had pooled in the body at the lowest points, succumbing to the whims of gravity. The flesh had darkened to a purplish black in those places, and Stan knew that shifting the body would risk the rupture of some weak point in the skin.

In his youth, he had cleaned up after many murders and fights. It was never pleasant, and he had no desire to do it again. At least not without the proper equipment, and he was unsure as to how much of what he needed was in the house.

"You are correct," Stan agreed after a moment. "There is no doubt now that the man is dead. I will take photographs and mail them to Mr. Pettigrew."

"And then you'll clean up the body?"

"Yes," Stan nodded. He walked to a metal wall locker, opened it and removed a Polaroid camera. "I must ask you to leave."

"Enjoy," Philomena chuckled and left the basement.

Stan removed a package of film from a lead-lined safe and prepared to take photographs for Mr. Pettigrew.

CHAPTER 45
NOT ANSEL ADAMS

Abigail walked into Ezra's office with the daily mail and smiled. "Any word from Robert, Mr. Pettigrew?"

"Nothing of terrible importance, I'm afraid," Ezra answered, pushing himself away from his desk and stretching. "He continues to wait for further instructions."

"Well, he certainly isn't splurging," she said, handing Ezra the mail. "Just the absolute basics for his meals. I wish he would eat a little more."

Ezra chuckled. "I'll be sure to pass that along to him, Abigail."

"Coffee, sir?"

Ezra glanced at the time, saw it was close to eleven in the morning and nodded. "Yes. But half decaf, if you could, please."

"Of course," she smiled and exited the room.

Ezra flipped through the mail, most of which consisted of fliers for different services he would never need, tree trimming, nail polishing, dog watching, etc. A single, slightly oversized yellow envelope caught his attention.

The return address was the factory in Mason, New Hampshire. Printed in neat, legible script were the words, *Photographs, please, do not bend.*

Ezra took his letter opener out of the desk drawer, slid the thin brass blade into a small gap and cut the envelope along the flap's fold. The sound of the paper tearing filled the room, and then Ezra put the letter opener away. He glanced in the envelope, saw what looked to be a note as well as Polaroid pictures, and shook it out onto the desktop.

Seven photos and the paper skidded out, and Ezra's heart skipped a beat.

Seven photos of Wiston's corpse looked up at him.

There was no mistaking the fact that the man was dead despite him still being tied to a chair.

The man, Ezra realized, had probably been dead when Stan had sent the original photo and message.

Ezra picked up the folded piece of white paper, opened it, and read the message written therein.

> *Mr. Pettigrew,*
> *As you can see, I have killed your assassin. In addition to this, I have removed all the*
> *ghosts you left in my town. It is my hope that your assassin did not have a family, for they*
> *will not have a body to bury. His remains will be scattered. Please understand you have*
> *done this. Also, please understand that I will kill anyone else you send here to harm us.*
>
> *Sincerely,*
> *Stan Owens*

Ezra Pettigrew was not a connoisseur of death. He had never fantasized about being in the military as a child or any other sort of violent activity. Ezra had, quite frankly, only ever been interested in business and making money. One ex-girlfriend, extremely literate, had gone so far as to refer to him as Ebeneezer Scrooge.

Ezra had needed to look up the reference to understand it. Reading, other than business reports and various management styles, had never interested him either.

The photographs of Winston's dead body were the proverbial car wreck. Ezra couldn't look away from them. Horrified, he spread them out and placed them in a rough order. Some were taken from a few feet away. Others were up close so Ezra could see massive, dark splotches along Winston's face where it pressed against a cement floor.

A knock sounded at the door and Ezra swept the photos off the desk and into a drawer.

Abigail entered, carrying his coffee and smiling. Yet the smile faded as she looked at him. She set the coffee down in front of him and asked, "What's wrong? Has something happened to Robert?"

Ezra shook his head, cleared his throat and said, "No. Nothing has happened to Robert, thankfully. I'm afraid that one of the pieces of mail, the one marked photos, contained exactly what it said. Photographs, but they were of Winston."

"Being held prisoner?" Abigail asked in a low voice.

Ezra shook his head. "No. I'm afraid they are photographs of his body."

Her eyes widened, and the color drained from her cheeks.

"This man, Stan Owens, he sent those to you?" she asked, her voice ragged.

"Yes," Ezra nodded.

"He's an animal," she whispered, shaking her head. "What kind of human being would do that? How can he live with himself?"

"I don't know," Ezra answered. "Some men are monsters, Abigail, and there's just no explaining it."

"Are you going to call Robert back? What if something happens to him? What if Owens finds him?"

"I will be speaking with Robert later," Ezra assured her. "When I do, we'll make plans to bring him back. I don't want to lose him any more than you do."

She nodded, tried to speak and then closed her mouth before leaving his office.

Ezra lifted his coffee mug, took a long drink of the hot liquid, and then set it back down. For a moment, he remained perfectly still. After a deep breath, he opened the desk drawer and removed the photographs.

He spread them out again and wondered what kind of man could kill like that.

CHAPTER 46

A HEAVY WEIGHT

They sat together, side by side, looking out over the water behind the Boys and Girls Club in Milford, New Hampshire. They sat on a picnic blanket, and the remnants of their meal had been tucked away into a woven basket. Stan's suitcoat was around Gwen's shoulders, and the sound of water formed a soft and gentle backdrop to the world.

"You seem preoccupied, Stan."

"I am having a difficult time," he admitted.

"Is there anything you need help with?"

Stan smiled at her, an unforced smile that he found strangely comforting. "Being with you is help enough, Gwen."

She kissed his cheek and grinned. "You say the sweetest things, and you're not even trying to get anything."

Stan frowned. "Why would I?"

Gwen laughed and stretched out on the blanket, resting her head in his lap and looking up at him.

"Tell me what's giving you a hard time, Stan."

He hesitated, then decided she was the only person he could tell.

"You know my friend Adam is in the hospital," he began.

"Yes."

"And you know I have a unique ability to speak with the dead. To see them," he continued.

"Yes."

"I was at the hospital not long ago, and I was met by the ghost of a young boy," Stan told her. "He was a pleasant child, and he knew I was Adam's friend. The boy told me Adam was close to death. Whether he dies or does not, no one knows. Adam could break from his coma, or he could succumb to death."

"How can he know that?" Gwen asked.

"There are times when a soul leaves the body before death," Stan stated. "It is, at times, referred to as a near-death experience. The dead can speak with Adam. I cannot. He is neither living nor dead when he is in a state of near-death."

"I'm sorry."

"As am I," Stan sighed. "Adam's current situation made me question my past. Why am I still here? Why am I alive and enjoying your company? I do not feel guilty, as though I should suffer. It is a question of whether there is any intelligent design in the universe. I did horrible things as a young man, Gwen. I was merciless and violent in ways most people cannot comprehend. Even now, when I reflect on my actions, I cannot find fault with myself, and that is wrong, is it not?"

"It's not." She shifted her position slightly to look at him better. "I've told you before, Stan, that you cannot be held accountable for what you did to survive in an extremely abusive environment. You were tortured, manipulated, and subjected to a living hell. Few people would survive such an experience. Fewer still would survive with any sort of moral compass intact. A fraction of that might survive and become what you are."

"What am I?" he asked, and he was surprised at the hoarseness in his voice.

"You are a protector, Stan Owens," Gwen told him. "Look at what you've done for Mason. You protect them from ghosts. You protect them from violence."

"By committing violence."

"Yes," she agreed. "By committing it. Do you enjoy it?"

"No."

"Have you tried other means?" she asked.

"Yes."

"Everyone in Mason knows you, Stan," she continued. "When we walk through town together, everyone says hello. You eat for free. People give you rides. All that happens because you are selfless. You put yourself in harm's way for others. They recognize this. I know you don't accept money for anything you do. Everyone knows it. That's why they take care of you. It's why you live for free at Marilyn's. It's why they feed you at the diner."

"It is my penance," Stan whispered. "I have done such terrible things, Gwen. I do not feel bad about them. I do not regret them."

"I know that." Gwen sat up. "I can't make you be at peace with yourself, Stan. I can help you. I want to help you. You're so important to me, I don't want you to be unhappy."

"You are important to me, too, Gwen. More than I can say."

"I know," she smiled. She placed her hands on either side of his face, pulled him in and kissed him full on the lips. When she broke it off, she winked at him. "I'm pretty sure if I didn't do that, you never would."

"You are right," Stan agreed, his face flush with heat. "I am a coward in more ways than one."

"That's not cowardice, Stan," she told him. "That's a whole lot of neurodivergence and childhood trauma. But I'm a big girl, and I don't have a problem taking the lead. Anytime you're uncomfortable, though, you need to tell me."

Stan brushed her cheek with the fingers of his right hand and enjoyed the softness of her skin. "I will tell you, although I do not think I will ever need to."

"I hope not."

She snuggled up against him, and they looked out over the water together. Off to the right, a heron stood in the shallows, seemingly ignorant of humanity around it.

Stan closed his eyes as his hand found Gwen's, and he did his best to ignore everything except her.

CHAPTER 47

THE RIGHT OR WRONG DECISION

Robert looked at the email from Mr. Pettigrew. It was short and to the point. Winston was dead. There was no question about it. Mr. Pettigrew wasn't sure what step he was going to take next, but he asked Robert to remain where he was.

Mr. Pettigrew also relayed a message from Abigail that she wanted Robert to eat more, and to be careful.

Mr. Pettigrew wanted Robert to be careful as well.

Robert did not.

Mr. Pettigrew was a good boss, a fine man who ensured that those closest to him were well provided for. If Robert's wife were still alive, if they had managed to finally have children, Mr. Pettigrew would have seen to their education. Of that, Robert had no doubt. Abigail had finished her master's in business administration, courtesy of Mr. Pettigrew.

He had also paid for Robert's several years earlier. The argument could be made that Mr. Pettigrew had only done it for his own self-interests, making sure that his business was run by people who knew what they were doing. That was true, but only to a degree. Unlike other employers, Mr. Pettigrew had not attached any strings to the education.

Neither Robert nor Abigail had been required to sign a contract stating they would stay for a specified period of time following the successful conclusion of their degrees.

They would, though.

They were loyal to Mr. Pettigrew, and they would remain by his side, regardless of the outcome. They were fully briefed on what it was

Mr. Pettigrew was attempting to accomplish with the utilization of ghosts. They knew why Stan Owens was a significant problem.

Robert and Abigail would stay until the end.

Standing up, Robert paced around his room for a few minutes, hands clasped behind his back, head bent slightly as he focused on his thoughts.

Stan Owens was a greater problem than they had believed he could be. The man was strong, resourceful, and well-liked in Mason. None of the ghosts had been able to stand up against him. And when Mr. Pettigrew had finally taken the gloves off and sent Winston in, that man had been taken prisoner and killed.

Robert couldn't understand that. Winston was a professional. A man who had made his living by ending the lives of others. How had a man in New Hampshire, and in a backwater town at that, captured and killed a man of Winston's caliber?

Luck.

It was the only thing that made any sort of sense.

Stan Owens was lucky.

Robert came to a stop, then walked over to the room's desk and took a seat.

He could understand, somewhat, how Stan Owens might have the ability to deal with the dead. Robert wasn't sure how ghosts operated, to begin with, so he could give some credence to the idea that there were people who can effectively eliminate or combat ghosts.

As for Stan and Winston, Robert could only imagine Stan had gotten the jump on the other man. A lucky punch, maybe two, and Winston would have been done.

But Robert knew how to fight.

He had boxed from the age of ten up until he had finished college at the age of twenty-two. He still went to the gym on a regular basis, a fact that Mr. Pettigrew was well aware of.

Robert knew he could get a jump on Stan Owens. The man was

older, slower, and, from what he had heard, perhaps a bit on the autistic side. All these factors could be played in such a way as to make it easy to take the man down.

Robert had no intention of killing Owens. He doubted he could bring himself to kill someone. But he could knock him out and hold him until Mr. Pettigrew could dispatch someone to take him off Robert's hands.

The dilemma was what would happen after.

Robert didn't think that Stan and Mr. Pettigrew would come to any sort of amicable agreement. He knew Mr. Pettigrew had ordered the death of one of Stan's friends, and combined with the death of Winston, well, that made for a poor base upon which to build any sort of relationship.

Robert didn't suspect, he knew with almost one hundred percent certainty, that Mr. Pettigrew would have Stan killed. Mr. Pettigrew was practical, and Stan was a liability to his business ventures as well as a threat to his life.

If Robert succeeded in incapacitating Stan Owens and then turned the man over to Mr. Pettigrew, it would be the same as if Robert had murdered Stan out on the street. This wasn't only in the eyes of the law, which would see him as an accessory to murder, but to his own morality.

Was Mr. Pettigrew's well-being worth damaging Robert's immortal soul?

"Yes," Robert murmured.

Opening his laptop, Robert accessed his email and drafted a short message to Mr. Pettigrew, one that he cc'd Abigail on.

> *Dear Mr. Pettigrew,*
> *By the time this reaches you, I should be in Mason. I believe that*
> *Mr. Owens has had a*
> *phenomenal run of good luck regarding Winston. I am confident*

that I will be able to capture Mr. Owens and hold him until such time as you might be able to take possession of him.
I will message you soon and give you an update on the situation.
It is my hope, Mr. Pettigrew, to message you with good news. If you do not hear from me,
then it means that I was incorrect in my assessment. Should that be the case, sir, I would like
to thank you for the many good years we have worked together.
Abigail, it has been a distinct pleasure. I believe all will work out well, and I hope we
might have dinner together when I return. If not, please know that I have enjoyed every minute of our time as coworkers.

I am your humble servant,
Robert Crisostos

Robert scheduled the email to be sent out three hours later. He sat for a short time, thinking of how best to enter Mason, how to find Stan if the man wasn't at his boarding house, and what to do once he did find him. They were serious, important questions, and so Robert spent a significant amount of time sitting and thinking.

Nearly an hour passed before he decided he had a workable plan. Standing up, Robert prepared to hunt down Stan Owens.

CHAPTER 48
BUTTERFLIES

The rocking chair had seen two hundred years of history, its rockers nearly worn flat over that time. Instead of a long and pleasant arc from front to back, the trip was short and often sharp, a reminder of how quickly a life could end.

It was one of the reasons why Gwen enjoyed the chair so much. Not for any dark or blighted sense of morality but because so many people had used the chair. On cool nights, such as this one, she enjoyed the idea that young and old had once sat in the rocker, that the owner might stand up and give it over to a guest. Parents had rocked children, grandparents had rocked grandchildren, and perhaps lovers, too, should they not put too much stress upon the wood.

Gwen ran her hands along the arms of the rocker, enjoying the smoothness created by generations of human flesh wearing down the wood. A dark patina stained the arms and brought her back to wondering who had sat in the chair and what they had done.

Did they read? Did they cross-stitch? Lecture or sleep? Did they die? Did they rock in order to ease the pain of forthcoming childbirth? Did they sit in the rocker and grieve the loss of a loved one?

They were questions she didn't have any answers for, and at times, she wondered if someone might be able to find out. There were some who could read the past just by touching an object, although they seemed to be few and far between. She knew there were others who, like Stan, could see the dead. But did Stan have the ability to read the history of the chair as well? Was it a packaged deal where he could see the ghosts, interact with them, and learn about them, all from a single item?

The thought of the man, who was never far from her mind, brought a broad, happy smile to her face.

Of all the classmates she could have thought of running into, Stan Owens had never been on the list. Nor had she thought she might find him in the least bit attractive. He had always been a quiet, unassuming young man. He had done his best to avoid being seen, but the girls had noticed. Stan had carried himself differently, and while it had been curious in high school and middle school, the truth of it was devastating.

Gwen closed her eyes against the horrors of his youth and young adult years.

He had told her some things, but there were more he kept to himself. She knew it was to spare her, but she had seen some of the scars.

Stan had pointed out the ones he had received from the wounding in Iraq.

But there were so many more. Crescent-shaped and cigarette-shaped, long, thin scars from razor blades and pinpricks in every major muscle group.

Gwen couldn't imagine how he had survived.

She opened her eyes and looked about her den. She missed him and wished he was sitting on her couch. He would be awkward and honest, and he wouldn't try to take advantage of her.

"And he doesn't have a phone," she chuckled.

But Gwen missed him. Missed the sound of his voice and the calmness that he exuded. He was a man undeniably comfortable with violence, and so, one who did not need to brag about what he could and would do.

She wondered, not for the first time, if she was falling in love with him.

He wasn't the man of her dreams, but that spot had last been occupied by Sebastian Bach, lead singer of Skid Row. She no longer knew what the man of her dreams might look like, but more and more, it was looking as though Stan might step into that role.

She smiled.

He looked like a good fit, as far as she was concerned.

And she knew she wasn't rushing into anything. Gwen didn't think you could rush into anything when Stan was involved. He moved at a steady pace. She knew herself well enough to understand there was no biological need for her to produce an offspring. Those days were long past, sacrificed to an emergency hysterectomy right after high school. She had not felt a compulsion to marry, much to her mother's chagrin.

Gwen stood up, stretched and removed her robe, draping it over the back of her rocker. She still had case notes to finish and enter, billing statements to submit, and emails to return. She wouldn't finish until close to midnight, but that wouldn't matter.

Work helped her think, and thinking helped her relax. By the time she shut down her computer, she would be ready for bed. It was a routine she enjoyed, and one, she realized, she wanted to share with Stan.

Butterflies fluttered in her stomach, and she came to a surprised stop.

She hadn't felt butterflies since before the hysterectomy, and that had been at the senior prom. In all honesty, Gwen hadn't thought she would experience that sort of reaction again.

But when she thought of Stan and some sort of life with him, her stomach twisted and turned, and the butterflies raced for her heart.

Smiling, Gwen went to the home office and set about her work. As she did so, she thought of Stan Owens, and her smile broadened.

CHAPTER 49

BERT DUPONT II

They weren't Marines, but they would do.

Bert Dupont II, no longer junior with the murder of his grandfather, stood with a trio of men from Derifield Construction. They worked together and had all gone to school together at Nashua North High School. When Bert had entered the Marine Corps, they had gone into business together, building houses in Southern New Hampshire. Dana, Erich and Geoff Mulvaney were large men, and they had no love for anyone who harmed Bert. As far as they were concerned, Bert was above reproach.

That was what being a veteran and their friend earned.

"You sure he's going to come by here?" Dana asked, spitting a thick glob of chew-stained spit onto the compacted dirt of the abandoned lot.

"Yup," Bert nodded. "Guy doesn't change his patterns or anything. You three up to it?"

"Of course we are," Dana snorted, and his brothers nodded. "We'll teach him, Bert, don't worry about that."

"I'm not," Bert replied, and the men shifted their focus to the sidewalk and waited for Stan Owens to pass by.

✳ ✳ ✳

Robert sat in his car, looking as though he was reading a book on his iPad.

In actuality, he was watching the street from four mini-cameras and a drone stationed in a hovering pattern above him. He had watched Stan long enough to know the man's walking route. It never varied, and every day, at two twelve in the afternoon, Stan walked down Olive Street.

Movement caught Robert's eyes, and he shifted the drone's camera to lock onto four men sitting in a vacant lot. Occasionally, one of them would glance up either side of the street as though they were waiting for someone else to join them.

Robert could only hope they would move along before Stan showed up. There was no way Robert could attempt a kidnapping in broad daylight. He didn't have the skills for that, and he knew it. The idea, though, that he might be thwarted by four idiots hanging out was a frustrating one.

Robert stiffened as he caught sight of Stan walking down the street.

The man wore his traditional outfit, a three-piece suit. His hands were clasped behind his back, head down slightly as though the weight of the world was born on his shoulders.

Robert hoped it was.

A yell caught his attention, and Robert watched as the four men stepped out onto the sidewalk a short distance from Stan Owens.

✳ ✳ ✳

"Remember me?" Bert demanded.

Stan Owens peered at him, then shook his head. "I do not. Should I?"

Bert felt his face redden. "You and me, we had a little fight at the VFW."

"Ah, yes," Owens nodded. "Now I remember. How are you feeling?"

Bert swore at him, and Owens shrugged.

Bert went to speak, but Owens interrupted him.

"I take it you and your three friends are here to threaten me with a beating?" Owens asked. "Or, considering their size, you believe you are going to give me a beating."

"Believe?" Bert asked, laughing. The Mulvaneys joined in, their deep chuckles filling the street. "We know. You got the jump on me in the VFW, I'll give you that. But we're going to give you that beat down now. The one you deserve."

"The one I deserve?" Owens asked.

An uncomfortable knot formed in Bert's stomach. Owens' tone had changed, a note of anger slipping in. A glance at the brothers showed they had not heard that change and that they were unaware of the sudden danger in the air around them.

"Tell me, Bert," Owens said, unbuttoning his suitcoat and shrugging it off, "how do you know what I deserve?"

Bert tried to answer but couldn't. He was fascinated by the sight of Owens draping his suitcoat over part of an old and weathered wrought iron fence.

"Are you going to gear down right here?" one of the Mulvaneys asked, causing his brothers to laugh.

"No," Stan replied. He removed his cufflinks, put them in the inner pocket of the suitcoat, and then rolled his sleeves up.

"Right, we don't need to wait for this anymore, Bert," Dana stated. "Come on, let's get it done with. I want a couple of beers."

The other Mulvaneys grunted their opinion, and as though controlled remotely, Bert walked stiffly toward Stan Owens.

✳ ✳ ✳

Robert knew a bit about fighting. He had studied fights where people had faced off against two or more opponents, and the rule for engagement was always the same.

Punch a hole in their line and get out.

No one could fight more than two people to victory. The movies painted a different picture, but Robert knew better.

These four men, they might get Stan Owens in the right frame of mind for Robert.

Grinning, Robert settled down to watch the show.

Not surprisingly, the four men spread out.

Stan slipped his hands into his pockets, then withdrew them, flexing his fingers.

Brass knuckles. Good for adding weight and power, they still wouldn't make a bit of difference against four men who towered over Stan. One of the men moved in, swung, and Stan Owens stepped in under the punch.

The jab that Stan threw was fast, hard, and Robert heard the man's ribs crack.

Then, the fight erupted, spreading across the feet as Stan Owens attacked the men who had tried to ambush him. His punches were hard and fast. He drove his elbows and knees into the bodies of the others. The brass knuckles broke bones and sent men dropping to the pavement.

Stan showed no pity.

No mercy.

When a man went down, Stan put the boots on him, stomping the man on the head before moving on to the next.

Within a matter of minutes, it was done.

Stan Owens stood in the center of the street, all four men in various positions spread out on the street in front of him. The man's shoulders were hunched, and a vicious, furious look filled his face and sent a deep, primal fear racing through Robert.

Robert knew, without any doubt, he wouldn't be able to fight Stan Owens.

He wouldn't have a chance.

Robert understood it wasn't luck that had brought down Winston.

It had been Stan Owens.

Stan Owens was simply terrifying.

Robert watched in silence as Owens straightened up, rolled down his sleeves, put his cufflinks back on and then retrieved his suitcoat. Birds sang, and animals called out as Stan put on the coat, buttoned up the front, and then, almost absently, returned the brass knuckles to his pockets.

Robert watched Owens walk away, considered calling 911 for the men unconscious on the pavement, and decided he didn't want to get involved.

He didn't want to get involved in the least.

And he had an email to write. He couldn't wait for emergency services.

CHAPTER 50
HIDING AWAY

Stan stood in the bathroom of 18 Maple Street.

He had killed the assassin in the kitchen.

His granduncle had kept a mistress here for decades.

Stan stripped down, taking the time to hang each item on a folder, then he placed his socks and other undergarments on the bed, laying them out.

He walked to the bathroom and ignored his own reflection. He knew what he looked like, and the scars brought back memories he did not wish to revisit. Neither those from Iraq, nor those from his childhood.

He turned on the shower, adjusted the water until it was the proper temperature, and then climbed in. Stan turned to face the showerhead, lowering his own and letting the warming water beat down upon him. He trembled, anger rising at the thought of the ambush he had disrupted.

No, disrupted was too mild a word.

He had destroyed it.

Stan had wanted to kill the men. All of them.

Not because they had thought to beat him; that didn't bother him. Not really. It was because they had interrupted him. He was heading to the house to think, not to shower. He could shower at Marilyn's, where his hygiene products waited. He could even have showered at Philomena's if he wanted to be berated by the dead woman as he cleaned himself.

No, all he wanted was to come and think about his next steps.

He had not yet heard from Shane Ryan regarding information on Ezra Pettigrew. There was no change in Adam's status at the hospital. There were no new attacks on any citizens of Mason or those passing through the town.

Had Ezra Pettigrew accepted the loss of the assassin, and would he thus withdraw from the town? Or was the man waiting to strike again, to send in more ghosts for Stan to challenge and drive out, destroy if necessary.

But he couldn't focus on them.

He couldn't focus on anything other than the black rage ripping through his body. His muscles tensed and relaxed, then tensed again. A deep, vicious urge to go back and kill them struggled to take control, and he fought it to the best of his ability.

The men had deserved a beating.

They did not deserve death.

Stan lifted his face up to the shower head, closing his eyes as the water struck his face and coursed down his body. Finally, the adrenaline dumped out of him, hitting his stomach and knotting it. He shivered despite the heat in the bathroom. A moment later, his stomach groaned and gurgled, and he felt the sudden urge to be sick.

He suppressed it. It was not his first run-in with adrenaline and its after-effects.

But they were never pleasant.

After the sickness passed, Stan turned the water off and straightened up. He took a large white towel from the linen closet, dried himself off and hung the towel up to dry over the mirror. He exited the bathroom and dressed quickly. A cup of tea and then a walk back home. That would be best. He longed for the comfort of the front parlor, where he could sit, drink his tea and read a book.

Perhaps, if he was lucky, Gwen might feel the need to call him.

At the thought of Gwen, the last bit of tension fled his shoulders, and Stan buttoned his suitcoat. He left the bedroom, went down to the kitchen and set water to boil. He would have a quick cup of tea for the walk home.

As he leaned against the counter to wait, he heard multiple sirens in the distance.

The injured men had been found. They would need to explain who beat them and why. He imagined that information would not be well-received in town, and he hoped the men he had beaten could leave without any further issues.

He had punished them enough. They didn't need any more.

Unless, of course, one of them said something stupid to the sheriff. Then, they would have to live with those consequences as well.

And that, Stan knew, was what most people didn't think of.

Consequences.

Stan did, though. He knew all about them and how they could happen to you, even when you had nothing to do with them.

Folding his arms over his chest, Stan lowered his head, closed his eyes and waited for the kettle to whistle.

There was nothing more important than that at the moment.

✳ ✳ ✳

Sheriff Paul Bowman stood at the back of the ambulance loaded with Bert Dupont II, Bert Senior's grandson. The young man had been beaten something fierce, and he looked at Paul with one eye swollen shut and the other glassy from an as yet undiagnosed concussion.

"Who did this?" Paul asked as the paramedic stepped out of the back for a moment.

Bert licked his lips, cleared his throat and whispered, "Stan Owens."

"What did you do to make him this mad?" Paul asked, unable to keep the surprise out of his voice.

"We were stupid," Bert admitted. "Shouldn't have done it. But we did."

"No, you shouldn't have."

"Won't do it again," Bert whispered, closing his one good eye. "Definitely won't do it again."

The paramedic returned, and Paul stepped back so the door could be closed.

In a few minutes, he and Analise stood alone. He glanced at the deputy, and she shook her head.

"Mulvaney brothers, well, the two who were conscious, said it was Stan Owens," Analise told him.

"So did Bert," Paul confirmed.

"Think they'll press charges?" she asked.

Paul shook his head. "Not a chance. They got a beating from a man almost twice their age and, more importantly, a man the town loves. They'll keep their mouths shut."

"Good," Analise said. "They deserved it."

"Yeah," Paul nodded. "That they did."

CHAPTER 51

A LITTLE CHAT

Ezra snatched the phone up from the table. "You're alive."

Robert replied with a weak laugh. "Yes, sir, that I am."

"What happened?" Ezra asked. "Did you find him? Did you try to confront him?"

"Finding Stan Owens isn't the problem," Robert answered. "He doesn't hide. There's no reason to. It's like all of Mason is his home. He's just moving from room to room. So, yes, I found him. As for did I confront him? No, sir, I did not."

"He bested Winston," Ezra remarked, trying to assuage any regret Robert might be feeling.

"Oh, I doubted that at first," Robert said with a weary chuckle. "I thought, wrongly, I might add, that Stan Owens had caught Winston off-guard. Perhaps scored a lucky hit that had incapacitated Winston."

"Did you learn what happened?" Ezra asked, surprised.

"No, I didn't," Robert replied.

"Ah." Ezra hid his disappointment.

"I have an idea, though," Robert said, and Ezra perked up.

Robert cleared his throat.

"I was following Owens," Robert started. "I had gotten his routine down and the places that he preferred to walk. I thought I could jump him at a good spot. Knock him out and then hold him until you can send someone to pick him up. A nice and simple plan. Those are the ones that work the best. But then, someone else showed up to ambush him. It looked like one of them wanted a little bit of payback for another fight. When I heard that, I thought I was getting lucky. These four men,

Mr. Pettigrew, three of them very large men, would easily beat Owens. How could they not? They were easily decades younger than him, in good physical condition, and spoiling for a fight."

"But that's not how it went?" Ezra asked.

Robert snorted a laugh. "No, sir, not at all. He tried to warn them. I'll give him that. When they ignored him, he took off his suitcoat cufflinks and then put on a pair of brass knuckles."

"Brass knuckles?" Ezra interrupted.

"Yes, sir," Robert confirmed.

"Was he able to use them?"

"Mr. Pettigrew," Robert began, his voice hoarse, "I've never seen anyone fight like that. No one. He was fast, and he was brutal. There weren't any wasted movements. It honestly looked like a choreographed fight out of a movie. That's how fast and seamless it was. I don't know the damage, but I can only assume that it was severe."

"How badly was Owens hurt?" Ezra asked.

Robert let out a harsh laugh. "Sir, they didn't land a finger on him. It was ridiculous. They should have. At least one of them should have. But they didn't."

Ezra stood up and paced the room.

"Robert," he said after a moment, "I want to know, do you think it is worth it to send in another gentleman to speak with Owens?"

"No," Robert answered without hesitation. "It is not. He'll either kill him or injure him too severely. It is not worth the financial risk, sir. Not in the least."

"Hmm, I've lost quite a bit in this venture to begin with. All right," Ezra sighed, rubbing the back of his head. "Stay in the hotel. Don't go out. Order room service for food, and send your clothing out to be cleaned. I'm going to be sending you instructions by tomorrow evening at the latest. You'll stay in the room for me?"

"Of course, sir," Robert responded.

"Good. Do your best to rest, Robert. You'll be back with us soon enough."

"Yes, sir."

Ezra ended the call and held the phone in his hand.

It was time to make a decision.

CHAPTER 52

REPERCUSSIONS

The town of Mason would suffer.

Some of those outside of the town would suffer as well, but that was an unfortunate side effect of Stan Owens' actions.

Owens would have to live with that, and Ezra would make certain to let Owens, and all of Mason for that matter, know who was to blame.

If the man had minded his own business, everything would have been fine. Ezra would have made his money, he would have sold the factory and moved on. Yes, he would have ruined the factory for a spell, but that was a fact of life when Ezra engaged in what he referred to as "strip mining" a business.

Was it unpleasant? At times, yes.

Was it necessary? If he wanted to make money, it most certainly was. And Ezra wanted to make money. He enjoyed it, even if he wasn't extravagant with it. Part of it was the challenge, of course. Could he buy the factory? Could he force the employees to go above and beyond? How much could he take from the company for the highest profit?

With the factory in Mason, he had suffered a loss, and all because of Stan Owens. Now, Owens was hunting him down via the internet, and Ezra's attempts to intimidate the people of Mason in an effort to cow Stan's investigation had failed.

Even the man Ezra had sent to kill Owens had failed.

So, now it was time to exercise an option Ezra realized he probably should have utilized first.

The physical destruction of the factory.

He knew for a fact that there wasn't insurance to cover the loss of wages for the employees. It would take months for New Hampshire's unemployment offices to come to the assistance of the suddenly unemployed factory workers. There would be a ripple effect as people lost their cars and homes due to an inability to make payments. Domestic abuse would increase, as would petty crime. Alcoholism and drug use would leap. There would even be a smattering of suicides.

Ezra had destroyed factories and communities before. He was well aware of the dangers and the fallout. It was an interesting social experiment, one he derived pleasure from watching.

Usually, he did it when he was in town.

Now, he would have to merely read the newspapers and watch the news coming out of New Hampshire. His only real dilemma at this point was how to destroy the factory. Normally, he would employ Winston or someone very much like him. With Stan Owens, however, Ezra didn't think that was a possibility.

Someone would notice strangers in town, and after the spat of deaths and attacks, Owens would eventually find out.

No, Ezra would need to use the dead, and he didn't feel comfortable reaching back out to Morrigan just yet. Her cold reception to the idea of making violent ghosts caused him to pull back slightly in their business dealings. It was clear she did not share the same philosophy, and in order to preserve any future dealings with her, Ezra had dropped the subject completely. He didn't want to purchase any additional violent ghosts from her, not when he still had two in reserve from when he had dealt with her predecessor.

He hadn't used them since his ignominious retreat from Mason, but he knew they would be up to the task. Lars Olafson and Hyacinth Gage could destroy the factory. Or, rather, Lars could destroy it while Hyacinth kept trouble away.

Ezra didn't think there would be too much interference so long as Stan Owens didn't see the dead.

With any luck, he wouldn't.

CHAPTER 53
ENDGAME

"Someone strange is in town," Sheriff Bowman told him.

Stan looked up from his book and at the sheriff. "Where are they?"

"He's parked in the lot at the factory," Sheriff Bowman answered. "Been there a bit."

Stan frowned. "Why do you suspect this person?"

"I've seen the car around a few times now, and he's not visiting anyone. Saw him in the diner, and he was listening to Analise, and me talk about you." Sheriff Bowman shook his head. "And I saw his car near the spot where you beat down Bert and the brothers. Something's not right with him."

"And you said he is at the factory?" Stan asked, placing his bookmark in the book.

"Ayuh."

Stan nodded, set the book down and stood up. He buttoned his suitcoat and asked, "May I trouble you for a ride, Sheriff?"

Robert sat in his car, the engine running and the lights off. The package sent to him by Mr. Pettigrew waited on the passenger seat. Robert had opened the package, made sure the two items were there, and then set it aside.

Only a few security lights shone around the factory. The building was closed, and a third shift was no longer operating. From what Robert had learned, the new owners had found it difficult to operate a second shift.

In a way, Robert felt bad about what was going to occur. In another, he didn't. The town of Mason, New Hampshire, had supported and continued to support Stan Owens. For that, they needed to be punished. And if that punishments was to be economically, then so be it.

The phone rang, and Robert answered it.

"Yes, sir?" he asked.

"Are you comfortable with this?" Mr. Pettigrew asked. It was a question he had asked a dozen times a day since he had told Robert the plan.

Robert smiled. "I am, sir. Tell me what to do."

"Exit your car and carry the package to the far right entrance. Once you are there, open each Faraday bag. When that is done, I want you to get back here as soon as possible. I'm not certain how long it's going to take Lars to destroy the factory, but I don't want to risk you."

"Are you sure he knows what he's doing?" Robert asked.

Mr. Pettigrew let out a rough chuckle. "Not at all. But I'm hoping he does. Come back as quickly as you can, Robert."

"I will, sir," he assured him.

Robert ended the call, picked up the box and left the warmth of the car.

✳ ✳ ✳

Stan stood in the darkness, just inside the tree line. He watched the stranger leave the car and carry a small box to the factory. The man hesitated for a moment, then squatted down and removed a pair of bags from the box. He fumbled around, straightened up, and then left.

As he did, Stan's attention shifted to the bags and the two ghosts who stood by them.

The car's lights turned on, and the stranger guided his vehicle out of the factory parking lot and onto the main road.

Stan looked at the ghosts for a moment, examining them. He had seen them before. The large blonde-haired man and the older, smaller woman.

They worked for, or were bound to, Ezra Pettigrew.

The dead man walked into the building, and the dead woman remained where she was.

A saboteur and a guard.

Stan walked out of the tree line and toward the dead woman. There was no going around her. Not if he was going to stop whatever they were planning on doing.

And he was angry.

Stan didn't want to go around her.

The dead woman saw him, watched him advance on her for a score or so of steps, and then realized he was walking toward her.

With a howl, she sprinted at him, leaping at the last moment. Stan planted his feet and braced himself for the impact which came a moment later.

Despite the iron encased in his flesh, the blow she delivered was still painful. It sent him staggering back even as it caused her to vanish.

But they were close enough to her object so that she was only gone for a few heartbeats. Yet, Stan still covered half the distance to the bags in that time.

The dead woman screamed and went at him again, avoiding his arms and trying to stop him with a plow to his ribs. He felt it. The cold sent ripples through him for a split second before his iron caused her to vanish again.

Pushing through the pain, Stan reached the bags and saw a lock of blonde hair and a gold ring on the ground beside them. Above him, the light attached to the side of the factory flickered, and the dead woman reappeared.

"Don't touch my ring!" she snarled, launching herself at him.

Stan braced himself and took the blow as he slipped his hands into his pockets and put on the brass knuckles. The dead woman's outraged scream dwindled away, but she reappeared a few seconds later, glaring at him as he knelt by her ring.

"This is yours?" he asked.

"What are you?" she hissed.

"Angry," Stan answered and smashed the ring with his brass knuckles.

The explosion threw him backward, fire singing his hair and clothes. His head rang, and the world shifted as he rolled onto his back. He tried to gather his thoughts, remembering that there was one more to deal with. One more ghost inside the building.

But the ghost wasn't in the building.

He stood above Stan, looking down at him with obvious confusion.

"Who are you?" the dead man asked. He looked around. "What have you done with Hyacinth?" The dead man stiffened, turned and shouted, "My hair is on fire!"

Stan managed to turn his head and see that the dead man spoke the truth.

The destruction of Hyacinth's ring and the resulting explosion had caused a flicker of flame to leap out. Stan could smell the unmistakable scent of burning hair, and he smiled.

"Put it out!" the dead man demanded.

"No," Stan answered, his voice coming out as a croak.

Furious, the dead man kicked Stan in the ribs, flipping him onto his stomach, but the ghost vanished as well.

The dead man was back within a moment, shrieking for Stan to put out the flames.

"No," Stan whispered, managing a single shake of his head.

The dead man kicked him again, and once more, disappeared.

Stan managed to turn his head toward the burning hair and saw it was nearly done for. The ghost reappeared, his incorporeal form falling apart. He opened his mouth to scream, and blue flames billowed out.

Stan closed his eyes and felt himself lift off the ground.

*** * ***

Robert hadn't gone directly back to the hotel.

In fact, he hadn't done more than move a little bit down the road to watch the destruction of the factory. He wanted to be able to report it directly to Mr. Pettigrew.

Robert wasn't going to be able to.

He watched, horrified, as Stan destroyed Hyacinth, then as the fire destroyed Lars, a second explosion occurred, and Stan Owens was thrown through the air.

For several minutes, Robert sat in the car, waiting to see if Owens would move. Waiting to see if the man was alive or dead.

When the sound of sirens and the flashing lights of the emergency vehicles pierced the night, Robert realized he had delayed too long. Throwing the car into gear, he tore off down a side road and made his way back to Nashua.

*** * ***

"The factory is still standing?" Ezra asked, keeping the disappointment and anger out of his voice.

"Yes, sir," Robert answered. Ezra could hear the exhaustion in the man's words.

"Have you slept at all, Robert?"

"Not enough," the man admitted.

"Alright, here's what I'm telling you to do," Ezra began. "I want you to rest tonight. By rest, I mean sleep. Purchase something to help if you need to. At eleven o'clock tomorrow morning, there will be a car there to pick you up and bring you home. You're traveling first class."

"Sir?" Robert asked, surprised.

Ezra smiled. "Yes, first class. You have gone above and beyond the call of duty with this assignment, Robert. When you're home, we'll have a long talk about what you saw and experienced, and then you'll take a vacation."

"Sir," Robert protested, "there's a lot of work I need to catch up on."

"And you will. But first, you're going to take a few days off. Not a week or two. I know you can't stand that," Ezra assured him. "But a few days. Then, when you come back, you'll be refreshed and happy to be back. I know. You have, after all, worked for me for quite some time, Robert."

"Yes, sir."

"Now, get some rest, and I'll see you when you get back," Ezra said.

He ended the call, put the phone on the desk and stood up. Pressing the heels of his hands into his eyes, he sighed and wondered what he was going to do next. He needed to wait until at least the morning to find out if Stan Owens had been killed fighting the ghosts, or hospitalized.

If Owens was still alive, would he give up on finding out where Ezra was?

They were questions he wanted answered, and he knew he wouldn't get them, not at least until the morning and possibly much later than that.

Ezra lowered his hands, stars flashing before his eyes.

He blinked, sighed again and put on his jacket. It was time to go home and leave his worries in the office.

If Stan Owens would let him.

CHAPTER 54

EDGEWOOD CEMETERY, NASHUA, NH

"Do you want me to wait here?" Gwen asked.

Stan shook his head, ignored the pain that flared up, and gave her a gentle smile, one that felt strange and out of place on him.

"No. I must meet with someone here," he explained again. "I do not know how long our conversation will last."

"You could call me," she winked. "If you had a cell phone."

"Indeed, I could," he replied and shifted his weight on the cane he needed now to stand.

Gwen slipped her arms around his waist, kissed him quickly on the lips and whispered, "Call me when you're back at Marilyn's."

"I will."

She kissed him again, then let go of his waist. She waved and walked back to her car. Stan watched her leave, turning left out of the cemetery and heading up toward Manchester and Concord Streets.

Stan turned his attention away from the street, saw a smattering of ghosts lingering about their graves, and started the long walk up to Anderson's Chapel. He took his time, stepping over the spots in the pavement where tree roots had broken through. He followed the winding road up toward the back of the chapel, which was where Shane Ryan had agreed to meet him.

Soon, the road curved and straightened, and there was Shane. The bald man sat in a folding chair, and beside him was another unoccupied chair. Smoke curled up from a cigarette dangling from the man's lips, and in his left hand, he held a bottle wrapped in a brown paper bag.

"Hello, Stan," Shane greeted. "You look terrible."

"I feel terrible," Stan admitted. He grunted as he sat down and then put the cane across his thighs.

"Want a drink?" Shane asked.

"What are you drinking?"

"Old English," Shane grinned.

"I do not think I will have much of a tolerance for malt liquor at this time."

"I'm reliving my wayward youth," Shane explained. "Without the violence and gunfights."

Stan nodded.

Shane took a final drag off the cigarette, stubbed out the butt and then placed it neatly on the arm of the chair. He drank from the bottle, set it between his legs, and absently picked up the butt, field-stripping it as he talked.

"You know," Shane began, "I don't understand people. This is a cemetery, right?"

"Correct."

"What do you have in a cemetery?" Shane asked.

"Graves and dead people," Stan stated.

"You see that berm on the right?"

Stan looked and nodded. The berm was difficult to miss, standing well over the six-foot high iron fence that wrapped around the cemetery.

"Well, a couple of years ago, the city needed to make room for more bodies. The cemetery owns all this. So, they cut down the trees that had been growing here, and the people around the cemetery complained."

Stan frowned. "About the trees being cut down?"

Shane nodded. "That, and now they had to look at the cemetery."

"The cemetery was here before their houses were built, correct?"

"The cemetery was here before any of them were born. There are graves from the late 1700s. Anyway, the point is, what kind of idiot buys a house next to a cemetery, then gets all mad because they needed to put more people in the ground?"

"I do not know," Stan answered.

"Rhetorical question," Shane muttered. "Sorry."

"I miss many rhetorical questions," Stan replied. "I apologize."

"Don't." Shane took a long drink, then fished out his cigarettes. He lit it and then exhaled the smoke out of his nostrils.

"Anyway," Shane continued, "that's off subject. I wanted to tell you that I have had absolutely zero luck finding out anything about Ezra Pettigrew."

Stan frowned and nodded. "He is a wealthy man. I do not doubt he has taken steps to hide himself from me."

"Yeah, I kind of figured that was the case," Shane grinned. "So, I reached out to a friend of mine. Well, he was a good friend until some rough stuff happened, but we've been working on it. He lives down in Connecticut, and he's an absolute genius with computers and finding out things he shouldn't. Kind of a hobby for him now. I gave him a call and explained what was going on. Explained why you needed his help, and he told me he'd be willing to help you."

"How much would he like for payment?" Stan asked.

Shane shook his head. "I told him your situation. What happened and how. He doesn't want any payment, Stan. He wants to help."

"How would we communicate?" Stan asked. "I do not own a computer, nor do I own a phone."

Shane winked. "I thought of that. You don't mind traveling, right?"

"That is correct."

"My friend lives in Connecticut, like I said. He's got an extra room, and you could stay there for the time it takes to dig up information on Ezra. Or the time it takes to figure out there's no way to dig up information on him. But, you could stay there for the time, work together and then, hopefully, do your thing."

"He does not have a problem with me seeking revenge?" Stan

asked.

"No," Shane answered, some of his playfulness fading away. "He doesn't have a problem at all. He's gotten his share of revenge, so he understands when people need to get theirs. He'll help you, Stan, because you need help."

"I will go to Connecticut and see him," Stan said. "What do I need to bring? Where is he?"

"Pack for a week or two," Shane replied. "Bring something to write with. As for where he is, he's not too far from Mystic, Connecticut. You can catch a train from Boston right to it. He'll meet you there. Just let me know when you want to go, and I'll bring you to Boston myself."

"Tomorrow?" Stan asked.

Shane grinned. "Sure. Why not?"

"What is your friend's name?"

"His name is Tom," Shane answered. "And he'll help you find Ezra Pettigrew."

Check out these best-selling series from our talented authors:

GHOST STORIES

RON RIPLEY
BERKLEY STREET SERIES
MOVING IN SERIES
HAUNTED COLLECTION SERIES
DEATH HUNTER SERIES

IAN FORTEY
JIGSAW OF SOULS SERIES
CULT OF THE ENDLESS NIGHT SERIES

SUPERNATURAL SUSPENSE

A. I. NASSER
SLAUGHTER SERIES
SIN SERIES

DAVID LONGHORN
NIGHTMARE SERIES
ASYLUM SERIES

SARA CLANCY
THE BELL WITCH SERIES
BANSHEE SERIES

For a complete list of our new releases and best-selling horror books, visit ScareStreet.com or scan the QR code below!

www.ingramcontent.com/pod-product-compliance
Lightning Source LLC
Chambersburg PA
CBHW050341030726
47503CB00008B/2558